FAKE THINGS

Damaged Devils #4

Charity Parkerson

Punk & Sissy Publications

—Warning: This book is intended for readers over the age of 18. Some of my books contain allusions to past abuse and trauma.

Editor: BZ Hercules & Consultants

Cover art: Temptation Creations

CONTENTS

Author Note	1
Introduction	2
Chapter One	4
Chapter Two	17
Chapter Three	36
Chapter Four	60
Chapter Five	82
Chapter Six	98
Chapter Seven	118
Chapter Eight	129

Chapter Nine   138

Chapter Ten   154

Chapter Eleven   167

Chapter Twelve   180

About the Author   195

Content   197

Author Note

This is a dark romance series filled with possible triggers. If you need a list, you can skip to the content warning after the About the Author page or check my website: charityp arkerson.com/damaged-devils

Introduction

BECOMING THE DEEP FAKE of a sitting senator was never part of Kenneth's life plan. Neither was falling for the detective bent on exposing him.

For most of his adult life, Kenneth has belonged to a crime lord. When his boss offers him a chance to transform into a missing sitting senator, he sees it as his chance to carve a new path for himself. Except the moment he gets his new assignment, Kenneth becomes an even bigger prisoner than ever before. The cameras and a local detective are always watching. One of those things is his new reason to live.

Detective Nic Higgins knows something isn't quite right with Senator Kenneth Yearly. He just can't figure out what. Every time he sets eyes on Kenneth, there's a feeling in his gut. Nic can't let it go. Unfortunately, curiosity isn't the only emotion the cold-hearted senator stirs in Nic, and the truth won't set him free.

Fake Things is the fourth book in Charity Parkerson's Damaged Devils series. These are dark romance stories with crime lords, assassins, and sociopaths who find their hearts. They are best enjoyed when read in order.

CHAPTER ONE

A CRINGE—LIKE WHEN HEARING nails on a chalkboard—went through Kenneth as Wendy pushed her empty coffee cup across the kitchen table. Kenneth's eye twitched. He didn't give her the attention she hoped to achieve. Before Kenneth had transformed into Senator Kenneth Yearly, his name had been Jared. Jared had felt sorry for Wendy Yearly. After all, the poor woman had been married to a psychopath in politician's clothing for nearly a decade. Now that Jared was Kenneth in every aspect that mattered, he hated her. He despised every breath she took. Kenneth saw her for the pathetic human she was. He didn't know how the real Kenneth hadn't killed her. Maybe he would have if the new Kenneth's organization hadn't killed the old Kenneth first. A smile tugged at Kenneth's lips. He fought a chuckle. Truth be told, he was a bit of a psychopath too. That was what made him perfect for this role.

"Why are you smiling at your phone? Who are you cheating on me with this time? You've already been through my son and some other guy half your age. What's this one's name? You know, so I'll know who plans to humiliate me next."

Kenneth drew a slow, steadying breath. His gaze lifted. He met the gaze of his bodyguard—another plant from his organization. They held each other's stare. King pulled out his gun behind Wendy. Kenneth bit back another smile and shook his head. King's shoulders fell. He put his gun away.

"I'm watching cat videos." He turned his phone so Wendy could see the device before he tucked it inside his shirt pocket. "But since you're hellbent on being humiliated, we should get divorced."

Panic crossed her features the way it always did when Kenneth brought up the inevitable. They had to shake her. It was past time for her to get out of the way. Now that he had won re-election, she had to go before she discovered he wasn't the man she had married. This was a better option for her. They could easily make her disappear.

"I'm too old to go back to work, and you've driven a wedge between my son and me. I don't have anything if I don't have you."

Kenneth fought hard not to roll his eyes. "You'll be fine. I'll have my lawyer get started on things."

"I'll tell everyone what you did to my son."

Kenneth kept talking, uncaring of her threats. Her son had disappeared two years ago. He wasn't coming back, and he wouldn't corroborate any claims she made. "I'll even let you have my second house in New York on Wisconsin Street."

"What house on Wisconsin Street? We only have the one house in New York."

A cruel smile twisted Kenneth's lips. His hatred for her rose to the surface, making him closer to the real Kenneth than ever before. "*I* have two houses in New York. The one we live in part time, and the one I bought on Wisconsin Street for Chad, so I could fuck him as loudly as I wanted, with no interference from you." Her expression almost made him regret the words. The original Kenneth had married Wendy years ago just to have her son. Chad had been an adult, and Yearly could have openly claimed him, but Senator Yearly had publicly been a staunch opponent of gays. Privately, he had fucked all the men. He hadn't been attached to any of them except Chad. Kenneth had died for that obsession. Now, he, the new Kenneth, had to deal with the fallout of the former senator's weaknesses. He wouldn't deal with this issue any longer. It was time for Wendy to face the truth and go.

A moment passed. Wendy's open hurt turned to calculation. The way he had known it would. "You've always said you'd leave me penniless. I can't afford to maintain a house."

Kenneth shrugged and stood. "Then sell it. We have an ironclad prenup. You'll get nothing else from me. You should be grateful for my willingness to do even that much." He had been prepared to offer money, but he hadn't realized old Kenneth had told her that. Kenneth couldn't afford to tip his hand by being more generous than his predecessor. He grabbed his jacket. "I'll have my attorney bring you the keys later today. You should prepare to be out by tomorrow." Kenneth paused while buttoning the suit jacket. "Sign the papers today, and the house I mentioned is yours. If you don't, then you'll get nothing. Your son is hiding from me for a reason. Follow his example and leave quietly. Otherwise, your silence will be permanent in every way."

The way Wendy gripped the edge of the table and held her tongue said a lot about the old Kenneth's cruelty. She already knew she had lost and believed him capable of anything. Again, he almost felt sorry for her. She had obviously endured a lot. But she had also turned her back on her son, who had been a victim of the man she had chosen to marry. In the end, her greediness would always win. He didn't doubt that would be true today too. She would sign those papers. Kenneth would finally be free. Well, as free as he would ever be now that he was trapped in this new life. He would take what he could get.

Nic checked his watch. It was eight thirty on the dot. He made a note on his phone. Kenneth always left at the same time every day to make his way through traffic to work. Nic didn't know what he hoped to learn by keeping meticulous notes on Kenneth's whereabouts when he was in town, but he hoped to spot something. Anything. He didn't know why he couldn't let this case go.

It had been his case. Months of wasted time and taxpayer dollars. Almost two years ago, Senator Yearly had fallen off the face of the planet. For several months, a team of FBI agents with Nic at the helm had searched tirelessly for the man. Then, right when Nic thought he had cracked the case, Yearly popped back up like a bad penny, acting as if no harm had been caused by his disappearance. For him, maybe no damage had been done. He had cake-walked his way through the next election. The man's wife hadn't even left him, even though he had very publicly announced he had disappeared because of an affair. Meanwhile, Nic had looked like a goddamn fool for treating the man's disappearance like a murder investigation. To his core, he knew something still wasn't quite right about the entire fiasco. Nic just couldn't decide what.

"Can we go now? We're supposed to be focusing on the Jefferson case. The Yearly case is closed. It's been closed. You need to let this go."

Nic tossed a quick look toward the passenger seat. Kurt had been his partner since the department closed the Yearly case. He had been assigned as Nic's babysitter. Everyone knew it was his punishment for challenging the senator, but no one said it. Maybe that was why he couldn't let this go. Honestly, that was only a tiny part of things.

"Let what go? I'm just working on case notes."

Kurt's eyebrow rose. Just the one. His brown eyes screamed Nic was a liar. "You had to stop to take notes about a different case right outside of the senator's house?"

Nic nodded. He refused to show an ounce of guilt. "If I have a thought, then I write it down. I'm a good detective because I refuse to forget a single detail."

Kurt snorted. He didn't call bullshit. Kurt couldn't force him to be honest, and they both knew it. It came down to the golden rule. Admit nothing.

Kenneth pulled from the driveway, and Nic followed.

"Are we tailing the guy now?"

Nic kept his eyes on Kenneth's car. "We're headed the same way, and this is a free country. Stop being paranoid."

"I'll add gaslighting to your list of transgressions," Kurt muttered under his breath.

Nic bit back a smile. One of these days, Kurt would loosen up and they would get along fine. That day likely wasn't today.

They stopped at a red light. Kenneth turned right. Nic didn't follow. If he did, he couldn't claim he wasn't tailing the guy. Nic swore he felt Kurt's stare boring into the side of his face, watching to see what he would do. Even though it made his eye twitch, Nic eased up, filling the spot where Kenneth's car had been. He would catch up with his prey again later when he was alone.

His cellphone rang.

Nic glanced at the dashboard touchscreen. It was his boss. He hit the phone icon on his steering wheel to answer. "Hello?"

"Why are you tailing the senator?"

Nic felt Kurt's I-told-you-so stare. "I'm not. I'm sitting at the corner of Clark and Palace, headed to question the father in the Jefferson case."

"That's funny. I just got a call from the senator's office, saying you were sitting outside his house again and following him to work."

"I told you where I am." Nic held his breath and waited.

"Detective Davies."

Kurt practically jumped to attention. "Yes, sir?"

"Have you been sitting outside the senator's house this morning?"

Kurt shot him a look that swore retribution. "No, sir. We're sitting at the corner of Clark and Palace."

"Mhmm." James' sound of disbelief felt damning in the otherwise silent car. "I expect a progress report this afternoon on the Jefferson case. Understood?"

"Yes, sir." Nic and Kurt spoke simultaneously.

The call ended without a goodbye. The light turned green. Nic eased off the brake.

"Listen—"

"Save it," Kurt said, interrupting him. "If you want to throw your career away on chasing Yearly, do it on your own time. I won't lie for you again. All it would take was one GPS check of our location and we'll both be fired."

"I know I—"

Kurt made a dismissive gesture. "I really don't want to hear it. Get fired on your own time. Leave me the fuck out of it."

Fair enough. Nic kept his gaze locked on the road and didn't say another word. Kurt was right. This was his obsession. He would have to take care of it with no witnesses. They weren't friends. He needed to remember it.

CHAPTER TWO

KENNETH STARED AT NOTHING, bored beyond words. It was almost funny. He had begged for this peace. Like most people in Archer Woods' organization, he had been raised as part of an assassin program. The crime lord who had taken him in and given him a job afterward was a good man by comparison. But working for Archer still hadn't meant peace. While Kenneth had no qualms about killing people, he craved riches without violence. When Archer's right-hand man Cree had put the idea of taking over the senator's life into Kenneth's head, Kenneth had thought he would finally have the life he wanted. Now he spent all day listening to whining old windbags as they sniped at each other. He supposed he was one of them now too. Thank God the original Kenneth Yearly had been vain. Otherwise, it would've been impossible to pull off the twenty-year difference between him and his predecessor. A surgeon might have ways to make him look older, but it hadn't been necessary. Kenneth shuddered at the thought.

By the time the session wrapped, Kenneth nearly ran from the building. Several people tried stopping him in an attempt to swing his vote. Kenneth kept his eyes locked on his goal: the door. He couldn't get out quickly enough. A thought hit and slowed his step. Where was he rushing to go? Hopefully, Wendy would be gone, but still. He couldn't do anything untoward. It wasn't like Kenneth could hit the bar or had any friends he could visit. Sometimes, at the oddest moments, everything hit him at once, suffocating him. This life was much lonelier than he had expected it to be.

"I wasn't following you this morning." A familiar form stepped into his path. Blue eyes held his stare. They were defiant. Something eased in Kenneth's chest.

"Detective Higgins." As Kenneth said the name, the darkness fled. Life handed him a challenge. He eyed the man's messy blond hair and wrinkled dress shirt. "It's always nice to see you. I don't recall accusing you of following me, but I certainly feel stalked now."

Fire flashed in Nic's eyes. "Your office called my boss, so someone accused me." He paused. "And I'm not stalking you. I'm talking to you."

Something about running into the detective always fired Kenneth's blood. He was the bit of excitement missing from Kenneth's life. "Well, if you're not stalking me and I didn't call your office, it sounds like someone else hopes to see you fired. Maybe we should go to dinner and discuss your list of enemies." The offer was a huge risk and just dumb as hell. Kenneth didn't want to go home.

Nic curled his nose. "I don't want to be seen with you."

"You're being seen with me right now," Kenneth shot back. "At least, if we're having dinner, it'll look as if we've buried the hatchet, and there's no need for your superiors to worry. Unless you have a personal reason, you don't want to be seen with me. Is it because I'm gay?"

The series of emotions that floated across Nic's face were comical as hell. He finally landed on furious. "Did you suffer a head injury in those months you were missing? First off, I don't like you. Your past stance on issues that matter to me sickens me. Not only that, but I'm gay, so fuck you for that one. You coming out after decades of spitting on the gay community doesn't magically absolve you of anything. Last but not least, you have a wife."

Kenneth never lost his smile. This was the best time he'd had in ages. "I asked you to join me for dinner. Not a date. I truly couldn't care less what you think of me, and as of noon today, I have no wife. We amicably signed our divorce papers and parted ways."

Nic blinked several times. "You'd think that would be all over the news."

"I imagine it will be once the press catches wind of things. There's really no story there, though. Obviously, I can't change who I am. It was time."

Nic's open confusion had Kenneth rethinking his offer. Dealing with Nic was always a risk. The man was smart. He knew something wasn't right with Kenneth. Too much time in Nic's company, and Nic might figure out his scheme. It was obvious there was already some puzzle inside his head that Nic furiously worked to solve.

Kenneth moved to step around Nic. "Good luck uncovering your work mole. I hope you find them before they sabotage your career." He made it two steps before Nic stepped into his path again.

Heads turned their way.

Nic looked around nervously at the people watching them. "Just dinner, right?"

An unhealthy wave of satisfaction ran through Kenneth. Something twisted rose inside him. Kenneth hadn't felt this reckless in a while. "Just dinner. No strings and no ulterior motive. We're just putting this bad blood to bed."

Nic still looked suspicious. When he finally nodded, Kenneth fought a triumphant smile from stretching his lips. He honestly had no plan and still it felt like a trap had sprung. Nic was as good as his.

Dinner with Kenneth was the dumbest fucking thing he had ever done. The only thing Nic could give himself any credit for being halfway smart about was refusing to ride with Kenneth. He followed him to the restaurant. As he pulled into the parking spot next to Kenneth's BMW, he still considered leaving. It wasn't too late yet to change his mind. Then he put the car in park and stepped out, stealing his own chance to run. It was like his body ran on autopilot.

Kenneth smiled. "I see you haven't lost your touch at tailing me."

"So you did call my boss?"

"It was a joke." Kenneth's confidence never dimmed in the face of Nic's irritation. It was obvious no one ever put the man in his place. Then again, his place was on top, so... fuck. Nic supposed he had every right to be cocky. Bastard. His light blue eyes and salt and pepper hair just screamed money, and it didn't even make sense.

Nic tore his gaze away from Kenneth and eyed the building. "I've never been here." In fact, Nic had never seen the place.

Kenneth motioned toward the door. "Then you're in for a treat."

The faster they went inside, the quicker this would end. Nic moved to the door. Kenneth reached past him and opened it. The scent of chocolate and spice washed over Nic. He nearly turned his head toward the smell. His stomach muscles clenched as if he braced himself to get fucked. Nic's reaction pissed him off. Nothing about the slimy senator could be considered the least bit redeemable. He forced himself to keep moving. His attention immediately shifted to the restaurant as he stepped through the door. The place was gorgeous... and empty. Almost like they were closed. That threw Nic. His gaze skirted across the room. Intimate tables with white tablecloths and flickering candles littered the place. Empty wine glasses waited to be filled. Polished silverware gleamed as the candlelight flickered from their shiny surfaces. Not a single table had any guests. A man in a black suit stepped from the recesses of the building as they cleared the door.

"Ah. Senator Yearly. I have your table ready."

All the tables looked ready. Nic fought a hysterical laugh. Kenneth set his hand on the small of Nic's back, as if urging him forward. Nic jumped away at his touch.

Confusion crossed Kenneth's features before quickly disappearing. "Sorry. It's a habit." He looked angry with himself as he barreled ahead, leaving Nic to follow. His reaction piqued Nic's curiosity. He wondered why such a habit irritated Kenneth to the point of needing to break it. Kenneth pulled out a chair, hesitated, and then pushed it back in before circling the table to sit. He looked mulish as he waited for Nic to claim the seat across from him. As he sat, it hit Nic. He had intended to pull the chair out for Nic before changing his mind. Kenneth fought good manners. That was odd. Then again, Nic had jumped away from his touch, so maybe not.

Nic tried moving past the strange moment. "What kind of food does this place serve?"

"Italian."

He even sounded mad.

"I love Italian."

Kenneth stared at a spot over Nic's shoulder. His jaw stayed set in a hard line. He didn't acknowledge Nic's statement. Nic fought to save the night. It was a hard pill to swallow, but Kenneth had been nothing but nice to him. Even this dinner was a career-saving move on Nic's behalf. Nic could try to be a bit more gracious. He opened his mouth, determined to say something nice, but nothing came to mind. Instead, he simply sat back and stared at Kenneth. In the past, it had occurred to him how young he looked for his age, but damn. He really looked young for his age. It was more than staying in shape, which he obviously did. He honestly looked no more than thirty-five despite the gray weaved through his hair.

Kenneth's light blue gaze finally moved his way, catching Nic staring. His features softened. Nic's heart skipped a beat for no reason at all. The room got hotter as they held each other's stare.

"So, that's a nice flower," Nic said, motioning toward a lone bright purple rose in a nearby vase.

A smile exploded across Kenneth's face at Nic's sad attempt at conversation. A breath caught in his throat. His mind blanked. He wanted to punch himself in the face.

"Tell me about yourself outside of detective work."

That was a good start. It was a lifeline. "Um. Let's see. I'm an only child. My dad passed a year ago and my mom moved to a retirement community shortly after. She lives on the west coast, so I don't see her often."

"You look too young for elderly parents."

Nic nodded. He got that a lot. "They waited until their forties to have me. They wanted to be financially secure. Mostly, I was just cheated out of time with them, but whatever. To each their own."

"What had you moving across the country? Or did they move?"

"It was me. I worked for a small county police department, but the FBI was my dream. I had to spend twenty weeks at Quantico as part of my training. Virginia actually has full seasons. I liked that, so when a post opened at the DC office, I worked my ass off to get it."

"I can read between the lines. You think I fucked that up for you?"

Like all his cases, and despite his personal feelings about the senator, Nic had cared about finding Kenneth. He had wanted Kenneth to be alive and well. Yet when he turned up exactly that way, Nic felt like a fool for caring. For searching. It had been his job, but still. It had been personal. He felt betrayed in some way he couldn't explain. All evidence pointed to Kenneth being dead. Then he wasn't. Something about the entire situation felt wrong. But there was a glaring truth he had to face before it cost him his career.

"You didn't fuck that up for me. My persistence did. When I took my team to New York, I was one hundred percent certain I had your killer. When you showed up alive and well, it was my inability to stop digging that lost me my team and got me bumped down. I should be thrilled you're alive. Most cases don't end that way." He couldn't explain why this one time it didn't feel like a win.

"If it makes you feel any better, those months I was missing were hell for me too."

Nic hadn't thought about it, but he supposed that was true. While Kenneth had left to be with his lover, he had ended up in rehab, fighting all the things that drove him to extremes. No one wanted to be an addict. Nic also imagined it was terrible to be closeted in his position. While it wasn't easy to put himself in Kenneth's shoes, he tried. Kenneth was older than him. He had lived in a different time when people weren't allowed to be out and in politics. Kenneth's father had been a senator too. Nic imagined expectations had been high for Kenneth. The pressure had to be immense.

"This is depressing. Let's talk about something else."

Before Nic could pick a topic, food appeared at their table. Nic stared at the plates of salad and lasagna. "We haven't ordered."

Kenneth smiled. "I ordered ahead. Trust me."

Even though Nic wanted to argue over Kenneth's obvious control tactics, he took a bite. It was as if the noodles melted on his tongue. "Oh, God."

Kenneth's smile turned wicked. His eyes flashed with something that had Nic taking a breath. "I told you."

"Holy shit." Nic took another bite. It was the most amazing food he had ever put in his mouth. "How have I never heard of this place?"

"It's not that well-known."

Nic focused on eating. Kenneth did too. Occasionally, their gazes met. They took turns being the first to look away. Nic had been out to eat with countless people over the years. This time, it felt like a date. He couldn't explain his reasoning. The night simply had an extra layer of nervousness and uncomfortably unspoken expectations. There were undertones. They ate and had wine.

Dessert appeared the way dinner had. It was cheesecake, so Nic didn't balk. Again, it was the best food he had ever eaten. Kenneth talked about everything and nothing. Nic listened. Several times, he laughed when Kenneth made flawless impressions of some of the politicians he worked with.

"You should've been an actor."

Kenneth's smile faltered. "That's what I wanted to be when I was a kid. I used to entertain the other kids in..." Kenneth seemed to realize he said too much. He cleared his throat. "I guess I should let you get home."

"I haven't paid for my dinner." And Nic wasn't ready to leave.

Kenneth stood. "They have my card on file. Places like this don't bring you the bill. It's considered poor taste."

"Oh." No wonder he hadn't heard of this place. "How much do I owe you?"

"I invited you, so I pay. You can buy next time." Laughter tinged the words like they were a joke.

Nic got it. They were an unlikely pair, but he didn't have the heart to joke. Despite everything, he had enjoyed himself. "Sounds good. Next time, I pick the place."

At his serious tone, Kenneth's expression turned solemn. He dipped his chin. "I look forward to it. Have a nice evening, detective." With another awkward dip of his chin, Kenneth headed for the door, leaving Nic behind.

Nic finished his wine to stop himself from watching Kenneth go. It had been the strangest night of Nic's life. He couldn't explain why, but he wanted to do it again.

CHAPTER THREE

THE PAPERWORK ON NIC'S desk blurred as memories of last night poured through his head. He had spent the entire night awake and poring over every detail. There had been nothing special about his dinner with Kenneth. So what was it? Nic didn't think he cared about Kenneth's position. Then again, power was sexy. No one was immune to that, whether or not they admitted it. Nic thought his fascination was with the flashes of vulnerability. There were moments Kenneth let his guard down. He didn't think Kenneth noticed, but Nic had.

"This came for you."

Nic glanced up as a guy from the files department set a vase on his desk. It held a single purple rose. In fact, Nic was almost certain the vase and rose were the table piece he had commented on last night.

"Where did this come from?"

The guy shrugged. "It was delivered earlier today. I don't know anything else." He kept moving, leaving Nic to stare at the flower. It was unique. He had never seen such a bright purple rose before. There could be no doubt it was the same flower. How had Kenneth done this? Had he paid the restaurant to pass it along? Had he delivered it himself?

Nic opened his drawer and pulled out a fingerprint kit. If anyone watched as he pulled prints from the vase, they didn't say anything. Nic was too engrossed in his own insanity to notice. He didn't know why it mattered so much who had delivered the vase, but he had to know.

After pulling all the prints from the vase, he turned his computer screen where no one could see it and pulled up Kenneth's file. He hoped his boss hadn't put an alert on the file to ping him if anyone accessed it again. Nic wouldn't be surprised since he had given his boss so much trouble over the case. To be safe, Nic found what he needed as quickly as possible. He jotted Kenneth's various numbers down and then closed the file. Nic hoped—if anyone was alerted—he could claim he had opened the file out of habit and closed it as soon as he realized.

With the info he needed at hand, Nic opened the case files for his current case so he would look busy. Then he started dialing, beginning with Kenneth's cellphone. To his surprise, it only rang twice before Kenneth's curt tone sounded in his ear.

"This is Yearly."

Since Kenneth hadn't technically said hello, Nic didn't either. "How did you get the flower?"

"Mhmm."

Holy shit. The hum went straight to Nic's groin. His stomach muscles clenched. He fought not to adjust himself in public.

"I hesitate to say I stole it. You might put me in handcuffs."

Fuck. He wanted to put him in handcuffs. Nic turned toward the wall and stared at his calendar, hoping to save himself. He didn't understand why this was happening. "I don't know. According to you, they have your card on file. You could probably take whatever you want."

A sexy chuckle caressed his ear. Nic's eyes fell closed. He took a slow breath. Kenneth kept talking while Nic savored a moment of guilt. "I know you only remarked on the flower to make conversation, but I still think the rose suits you. It's unique."

A smile snapped to Nic's lips. He liked the thought of being different. "Yeah, I'm sure I'm nothing like the people you usually spend your days rubbing elbows with."

"You say that like it's a bad thing. I spend my day surrounded by pompous old windbags who take legal bribes. Being different from that is a nice change."

"Then you should spend more time with me. I owe you dinner." Nic covered his eyes. What was wrong with him? This was the dumbest shit.

"Just tell me when and where."

"How about I pick you up at seven?" He chewed the side of his nail. A small part of him hoped Kenneth said no. It wasn't like Kenneth was a criminal or anything. There was no conflict of interest. Somehow, it still felt that way. He had spent so much time studying Kenneth's case and everything was just terrible timing. Nic didn't know why they were having this conversation.

"I'll see you then."

Nic took a breath. "Okay."

"Have a good day."

Damn. Why did Kenneth sound so sexy? "You too." The phone disconnected and Nic dropped his forehead onto his desk with a thump. Now he had to figure out where to take a goddamn senator to dinner. What had he done?

The house was blissfully quiet without Wendy. Without her there, Kenneth had dived headlong into full-on nosiness. He got a strange thrill from digging through old Kenneth's things. He had inherited someone else's life. Studying the old senator's life was one thing, pawing through his most personal belongings was another. The guy had a sickening amount of homemade porn in his safe. Kenneth had only watched enough to know they were all of Wendy's adult son. They were also pretty fucking heartbreaking. While Wendy's son Chad now owned the biggest porn production company in the country, it was obvious exactly whose hands had twisted him. Chad should have been the one to kill his stepfather. Luckily, knowing who took him out, Kenneth knew the man hadn't gotten a pleasant death. So there was some comfort there.

There was so much shit in one house, Kenneth didn't think he would ever see it all. Then there was also the house in New York. It was even bigger than this one. Kenneth felt defeated by it all sometimes. As a child, he had owned nothing. All he had known was abuse and hunger. Seeing so much unnecessary shit felt like disgusting excess. But then Kenneth would sit outside by the pool, with the moonlight highlighting the perfect landscaping, and a peace would settle into his soul. Unlike his predecessor, Kenneth appreciated this. He recognized how much more he had than most. It felt good.

The doorbell rang, and Kenneth checked his watch. Seven o'clock had sneaked up on him. Kenneth snuffed his cigar and headed inside. When he opened the front door, an odd sensation stirred in his stomach.

"Hi."

Damn. Nic sounded breathless. Kenneth wanted to make him do it again. "Hey."

"Um. Did you know there are reporters in your driveway?"

Fuck. "Yeah. Sorry about that. It seems someone at the courthouse saw my divorce papers when they were filed and leaked it to the media." He stepped back, letting Nic inside. "So, I was thinking. How do you feel about ordering in?"

Nic looked oddly relieved. His shoulders visibly relaxed. "That sounds great. Honestly, I was kind of dreading fighting my way back through the crowd. Just tell me what you'd like, and I'll order it."

Damn. He was obviously in a hurry. "Would you like a tour first?"

A sexy smile snapped to Nic's lips. "Sure."

Kenneth motioned Nic ahead of him. "Through here is the sitting room." While Nic eyed the expensive furniture, Kenneth eyed him. The ends of his hair were wet, as if he had just showered. White jeans cupped his round ass, and a red t-shirt molded his torso. He made Kenneth's mouth water. Nic headed for the door Kenneth had left open when the doorbell rang. He poked his head outside.

"Oh, wow. This is gorgeous."

Something funny happened to Kenneth's chest. It felt odd for Nic to immediately gravitate toward Kenneth's favorite spot. "That's where I spend most of my time. Obviously. That's why the door was open."

Nic stepped outside.

Kenneth followed. He watched Nic look around, seeing what he saw. The pool lit the backyard. A waterfall poured from fake rocks, keeping the pool's water moving. Strategic landscaping made it seem like a jungle. Tropical flowers scented the air. The tall fence kept them completely hidden from the world. Until that moment, Kenneth hadn't realized how romantic the spot seemed. He had always enjoyed the peace. The spot felt completely different with Nic there.

"We should eat out here."

Kenneth smiled at the idea. "Agreed. Give me just a second." He pulled his phone from his pocket and found King's number. He hit the phone icon and pressed the device to his ear. King answered on the first ring.

"Yep."

Kenneth fought the urge to shake his head at King's greeting. "Nic is here."

Nic's eyebrows rose, but he didn't say a word.

"On it." The phone disconnected in his ear.

Kenneth set the device on the nearby table. "I knew there was no way we'd get to have a peaceful night out, so..."

Nic's sexy smile had Kenneth incapable of looking away. "So... what?"

"You'll see. Sit with me."

They each grabbed a chair and sat. Before Nic could ask anything else, King stepped outside carrying two plastic bags. He set them on the table without making eye contact before leaving them alone again.

Nic stared at the King until he couldn't see him anymore. "Who was that?"

"An employee. Tonight, I got us Mexican."

Nic's gaze snapped to Kenneth's face. "I thought it was my turn to buy."

A smile that felt evil stretched Kenneth's lips. "I guess you'll have to see me twice more."

The way Nic shook his head and visibly fought a smile tugged at Kenneth's heart. "Mexican, huh? I won't be so easily wowed this time. Mexican is my favorite, so I'm hypercritical."

"I'm not concerned." Kenneth pulled out the aluminum containers and arranged them on the table. "Mexican is my favorite too, so I've become a bit of a snob about it." He pulled a six-pack of glass bottles from the bag. "And, of course, orange soda."

A laugh burst from Nic as he accepted a bottle. "Holy shit. I haven't had orange soda since I was a kid."

Kenneth nodded. "When I was a kid, it was my favorite, but it was rare for me to get it. It's likely one of the more ridiculous things I used to dream about having all I wanted one day." Nic laughed and Kenneth kept going. He enjoyed having Nic as his one-man audience. "I would daydream about having one of those tiny refrigerators in my bedroom. In my head, I would stock it with all my favorite things." Kenneth stared at his drink, seeing nothing but the past. "Fake things. That's how I survived." That was still how he survived.

"It sounds strange to hear that someone raised in so much wealth had the same fantasy I had as a poor kid."

Kenneth shook his head. Nic always made him forget he wasn't Jared anymore. He hated having to save the moment with a lie. "I wasn't given everything. My parents were hard people who believed in strict discipline. They were zealots. I guess that's why I spent the best years of my life hiding everything about myself they would've hated."

Nic nodded. He looked surprisingly sympathetic. "Like I said last night, my parents were older when they had me. They were extremely old-fashioned. Dad died never knowing I'm gay, and I was grateful for that. That probably makes me sound like a bad son or a coward, but I just couldn't find the words. When you grow up in a house with nothing but negative talk toward anyone or anything different, it's hard to be different."

"What about your mom? Does she know?"

Nic shrugged. "Probably, but I still haven't ever said the words to her. I've always just figured it wasn't important. She lives on a different coast, and I haven't made time for relationships anyhow."

"Really?" That shocked Kenneth. He expected Nic would be fighting men off all hours of the day. "How old are you? Surely, you've had at least one serious relationship."

A sexy chuckle slipped from Nic's lips. He popped the lid on his food and sniffed. "I'm thirty-six. Damn. A queso-covered burrito. It's like you're a mind reader."

"Ah. The subject change. You've had an ugly relationship."

Nic snorted. "Hasn't everyone?"

Kenneth didn't know how to respond, because no. He hadn't. Not really, but then it looked that way right now in his very fake life. But the man Kenneth had been before becoming Kenneth hadn't had time for that bullshit. He had been trying to survive. His life had been secretive. Dangerous. Still was, if he was honest with himself.

"I'll let you keep your secrets." Maybe Nic would let him keep his too.

Kenneth popped the lid on his dish and splashed some hot sauce on top. He focused on eating so Nic could too. Three bites in,

Nic finally broke the silence. "He was five years younger than me and completely unfettered by reality."

Unfettered by reality. Kenneth liked that. "How so?"

Nic kept his gaze locked on his food. "He was young and pretty. Life was always easy for him. People always just gave him whatever he wanted if he smiled enough. He didn't understand why I had to work. Why did I have to travel? Couldn't someone else at another department do that? He liked telling people his boyfriend was an FBI agent, but he didn't want me to actually work the job. I tried really hard to balance things, but it was never enough."

"What was his name?"

"Chaos."

Kenneth stopped eating. "Are you being serious?"

Nic snorted out a laugh. "Yes."

Laughter burst from Kenneth without his permission. "Yeah. No one named Chaos has ever worked for anything."

They exchanged a glance and burst into laughter.

Nic swiped at his eyes. "You know, I didn't expect to like you."

"I didn't expect to like you either."

They both visibly fought not to exchange another glance. Kenneth took a drink. Their eyes met. Kenneth had to cover his mouth to keep from spewing orange soda all over their food. It was nice. He hadn't felt so free in ages. Kenneth wanted more.

Hot water poured down Nic's body. He tried not to think about his night, but it was all he thought about. They had talked for hours. Nic had forgotten he had to work tomorrow. He had forgotten everything. Kenneth wasn't at all what Nic expected. He was down to earth and nice. The guy was fucking insightful as hell and funny. God, he was so funny. Halfway through the night, Nic found himself incapable of looking at anything other than Kenneth's lips and eyes. A craving had built to an insane level. Then the night had ended, and Kenneth hadn't as much as hugged him. They had shaken hands, for fuck's sake. Like business associates. Goddamn. That ate at Nic. He should let this go.

Nic stepped from the shower and dried his skin. He tried extra hard to keep his mind blank. Nic grabbed his underwear and pulled it on, determined to go to bed with an empty brain. He gathered his dirty clothes from the floor. As he lifted his pants, a piece of paper fell from his back pocket. Confusion had him setting the clothes aside and unfolding the note. He hadn't even noticed anything in his pockets and Nic definitely hadn't put it there.

His gaze slid across the paper. A smile stretched his lips.

I think you're incredibly sexy, but I don't want to make you uncomfortable. You can see me again as friends, and that'll be fine. I'm good with being a friend. I need that too. But if you're interested in more, I have to head to Massachusetts this weekend. You should come with me.

—Ken

Nic bit his bottom lip. Kenneth was smooth as fuck. They had been together all night, and he hadn't seen Kenneth write any note. He definitely hadn't felt that note being slipped into his back pocket.

Aimlessly, Nic padded from the bathroom while still staring at the scrawled words. He moved to the desk in his bedroom and sat. Nic leaned back in his chair and focused on his black computer screen while seeing nothing. With his mind on lockdown, he woke his computer and opened the file he had been secretly building on Kenneth. He pulled up his latest surveillance video. Kenneth sat alone at an outdoor cafe. Too many times, the video zoomed in on Kenneth's face. Nic had the same thoughts now as he'd had then. Kenneth looked unhappy.

At the time of taking the video, Nic hadn't cared. He assumed the guy's wife made him miserable after the disappearing and cheating scandal. Now he knew the stories of Kenneth hiding and suffocating. Nic paused the recording on Kenneth's face. Sometimes, he felt suffocated too. He had been climbing in his career, neglecting his personal life to do so, only to have this one case become such a deep obsession that it stole his future from him. Now he wondered if his passion to solve this case hadn't actually been infatuation with the man at the center of it all. While he didn't think that was true, he still questioned himself.

There was no denying those full, gorgeous lips wiped his mind. Those light-colored eyes seemed to see all the way to the depths of Nic's soul. There was something happening between them. Unfortunately, there was a very good possibility it might destroy his career. He couldn't give a valid reason for that deep-seated belief, but it was there. Nic's mind stuck on repeat as the image of

Kenneth's heated stare infiltrated his brain and set up shop. At one point, Kenneth had sipped his drink and then licked his lips. Nic had gone hard, then fought to hide it. He didn't recall the cold senator being this fucking sexual. Now that Nic had noticed, he couldn't stop. The way Kenneth stared at Nic was addicting. He wanted more. Nic craved it.

His hand slid south as he stared at Kenneth's image. He needed to know what those lips felt like wrapped around his cock. Nic set his erection free and stroked. Kenneth had been hiding his sexuality for decades. Would that repression make him wild on Nic's dick?

"Fuck."

He wanted to know. Nic stroked faster. He gripped the edge of the desk and gasped for air. Pressure climbed his shaft. Nic held his breath. His gaze never wavered from Kenneth's face. Nic's obsession had him closer to the edge, faster than ever before. He longed to paint Kenneth's full lips with his cum. When the orgasm hit, Nic cried Kenneth's name. Even as he stroked out the last drops of cum, no regret hit. That was answer enough for him. He would go to Massachusetts with Kenneth. One weekend. He had to know. Nic had to have him.

CHAPTER FOUR

A QUICK PRIVATE FLIGHT had taken them to Massachusetts, where Kenneth had arranged for a car before their arrival. He swore he felt Nic's nervousness every mile of their trip. Kenneth didn't know how to set him at ease.

"It's really beautiful here. I can't stop staring at all these trees."

Kenneth nodded but kept his eyes locked on the road. "It's peaceful. I started coming here a few years ago to wind down on long weekends and whatnot. It's a great place to get lost."

"Is that what we're doing this weekend?"

A smile snapped to Kenneth's lips. "Yes, and no. At some point this weekend, I have to meet with a land developer who hopes to expand into New York. He wants to convince me to smooth the way for him."

"Do you take bribes?"

Kenneth snorted. "There isn't a politician alive who isn't getting wined and dined by someone. It's unavoidable. I'm in the position they need. They think they can ease the way with the right amount of perks. But—at the end of the day—it doesn't work that way. Their interests have to align with the best interests of my state. Otherwise, I'd never get re-elected." He flashed Nic a smile. "Obviously, I easily did that, so I must be doing something right."

It was all bullshit, of course. Archer had bought the election and Kenneth didn't have the luxury of thinking about New York. He did what was best for Archer and no one else. Archer needed land for warehouses. Those warehouses would hold guns, stolen cars, and whatever else Archer needed. In New York, they would be located in the perfect spot to easily flood the streets without traveling long distances to the city. There were farms on the edge of the city that would sell for the right price. Kenneth hoped to pitch the idea to his state with the promise of jobs coming to the area. That would give Archer breaks on the legal side of things such as taxes and whatnot. No one was completely immune from the IRS. Archer had to look legit on the surface. He excelled at that part. That was why Archer did so well as a crime lord. When it counted, he looked completely above board.

Kenneth tried to move on from talking about work. "Anyhow, my meeting should only take two hours, tops. That leaves me with an entire weekend to relax and focus on you."

Nic didn't respond.

Kenneth stole a quick glance his way. Nic silently watched him with enough heat to make Kenneth lose his breath. He focused on the road. His thoughts raced. When Nic had texted him, agreeing to this weekend, Kenneth had expected a bit of a pushback. He imagined Nic felt the same unwanted attraction Kenneth felt. It was odd for a lot of reasons. For one, they had always felt like they were on opposite sides. In a way, they were. Kenneth was a criminal. Not that Nic knew that. For another, Kenneth had been surgically remade to look like a man over twenty years older than him. While the original Kenneth Yearly had—thankfully—looked much younger than his age of fifty-seven, Nic still believed him to be fifty-seven. In reality, Kenneth was a year younger than Nic. Kenneth hadn't expected this kind of complication in his life. He had promised Archer six years. For the next six years, he would play the senator, working out his term. Then Archer would find a real senator with real qualifications. Afterward, Kenneth could retire and disappear. If he wanted, he could reverse his surgery and go back to being Jared. He would have Kenneth's money and be free. Right now, he felt the invisible chains. They were heavier than ever.

"I've never seen you nervous. You're usually annoyingly cocky."

Kenneth scrambled for a lie at Nic's observation. "I guess—if I'm being honest—I never expected you to be genuinely attracted to me. I'm a lot older than you."

God. Everything inside him rebelled against those words.

"That guy you disappeared with for months was around my age."

Fuck. Things kept getting worse. Every lie he told was a stumbling block for the future. Archer had made it look like Kenneth had disappeared with the man who had actually killed him. Too many things could go wrong from here. "Yeah, well. That wasn't exactly a healthy relationship, was it?"

A soft, sexy-sounding chuckle rumbled from Nic. "I guess that's true since I saw an image of him leading from your house with what looked to be a bloody sledgehammer."

Kenneth cringed inside. "Just a bit of role play that turned into an escape plan. It's not easy having your every move fodder for the masses. I just wanted to be free. Have you ever felt that way?"

Nic didn't answer right away. When he finally spoke, he sounded sad. "Honestly? I've felt that way a lot lately."

Guilt washed over Kenneth. He understood what Nic didn't say. It was Kenneth's fault. His career had taken a hit by Kenneth turning up alive and well while Nic had been investigating his murder. Now, the dreams he had were all but dead. His prospects for climbing the FBI ladder were low. That was on Kenneth. More so than Nic would ever know.

He tried lightening the mood. "For a weekend, you get to be just you. Not Detective Higgins. Just Nic."

To Kenneth's surprise, Nic took his hand. "And you get to be just Kenneth."

"Yikes."

A sexy rumble of laughter caressed Kenneth's ears. "I don't know. So far, I've really enjoyed spending time with you when you're just being you. I actually like that version of you."

"Actually?"

Another chuckle filled the car. "Yes, actually. I didn't like you at all before spending time with you. You're not what I expected."

Truthfully, that warmed Kenneth's heart. That meant Nic liked the real version of Kenneth. That mattered. Nic was right. For one weekend, Kenneth would just be himself. Honestly, he couldn't wait.

Damn. Nic really liked this version of Kenneth. Every hint of nervousness he showed made Nic a little more desperate to fuck him. God. How had he gotten here? Kenneth kept casting looks Nic's way. He didn't pull his hand away, but he looked unsure as hell. Having Kenneth off balance fed something dark in Nic's soul. He hadn't thought about it, but it had been some time since he last had sex. Kenneth was the first person to catch his attention in a long time. He had been too busy to even think. That was over.

Kenneth turned left and headed down a long driveway. It took a minute, but finally, a two-story home that looked like it was more windows than walls came into view. The place was gorgeous. He could already see the pool and a huge pond in the distance.

"This is gorgeous."

"It belongs to a friend."

Damn. It must be nice to have friends who loaned whole-ass houses for the weekend. Nic kept that thought to himself. He recognized now part of his problem with Kenneth was the wealth. Nic didn't think he was jealous. He just hadn't met a rich person he liked. It didn't look like he could say that anymore.

Kenneth parked. They climbed from the car. Kenneth beat him to the back to grab their bags. Nic tried to grab his, but Kenneth walked away with both suitcases, leaving Nic to close the back. With a shake of his head, Nic followed on Kenneth's heels. That feeling of something being off about Kenneth overcame him again. It didn't give him a bad vibe or anything. There was just some revelation right out of his reach. The detective inside of him wanted to dig until he found every secret Kenneth held. There was something about his mannerisms Nic couldn't discern.

Then they were inside, and Kenneth set their bags aside. Something inside Nic roared to life the second he closed the door, shutting them away from the world. He molded against Kenneth's back and kissed the side of his neck. It felt like breathing. That was how natural it was for him to touch Kenneth.

Kenneth hummed.

Nic's arms encircled him. He ran his hands up Kenneth's torso. Damn. It was solid beneath his touch. His nipples were hard.

Kenneth turned. Their mouths met. The entire world disappeared. Kenneth's tongue slid across his and Nic melted. Nic's fingers found the hem of Kenneth's shirt and dove underneath.

Kenneth backed away. "Maybe we should slow down."

Disappointment washed over Nic, but he got it. Kenneth hadn't been out that long.

This was probably too much, too fast. "Okay. Do you want to show me around?"

For a moment, Kenneth stared at him in silence. He looked as disappointed as Nic felt. Then the space between them vanished again as Kenneth overcame him. Their mouths met and clashed. Kenneth's hands were everywhere. Nic lost himself to the competing sensations. He hadn't realized how touch-starved he had been until he found himself beneath Kenneth's hands.

Kenneth maneuvered him toward the couch until Nic found himself seated, with Kenneth straddling his lap. When Nic had made his move, he hadn't expected to get this far. He was happy to just taste Kenneth's tongue.

Because he—strangely—cared about Kenneth's feelings. He tried slowing things down without giving up completely. His kiss softened. He kept his touch loving rather than groping. Nic felt Kenneth's muscles relax. He melted into Nic while openly savoring Nic's tongue.

Nic stroked his back, luring Kenneth into his web. He didn't want to scare Kenneth with his intensity. Sometimes, Nic could be too forceful. He knew that. Nic had always had a bit of a bulldog attitude. He tended to charge at everything. Kenneth hadn't lived the same life as him. He needed a softer hand. Nic didn't know how he knew, but he did. This man had more reasons than religion to fear his sexuality. Someone had been too rough with him. That was what Nic had seen in his eyes when Kenneth begged to slow down. They had all weekend.

"I want you to fuck me."

Or they could do this right now. "Point me toward the bedroom."

Kenneth slipped from Nic's lap, but instead of leading Nic to the bed, he dropped to his knees.

Nic watched—frozen with lust—as Kenneth reached for his zipper. He let Kenneth open his pants. The hungry expression Kenneth wore kept Nic on edge. Kenneth set Nic's erection free. Nic couldn't look away from the flush on Kenneth's cheeks or the way his lips looked after Nic's kiss. He genuinely wanted Nic. Something stirred in Nic's chest. The truth hit him. He wanted more than one weekend. As hard as he had fought his attraction to Kenneth, Nic recognized why now. Kenneth wasn't some hot guy he met in a club or on an app. He was the once-in-a-lifetime guy. Kenneth was the one that anyone with any sense wouldn't let get away.

Nic stopped Kenneth before he went down on him. He took Kenneth's hands and came to his feet, pulling Kenneth to his as he went. "Take me to bed."

Kenneth's lips parted in surprise. His gaze moved over Nic's features. Finally, he turned away and headed down the hall with Nic's hand still held in his. As they headed through an open door, Nic barely spared a glance for the wealth surrounding them. Everything was navy and gold, with splashes of white.

At the edge of the king-sized bed, Kenneth pulled him to a stop and went to work, undressing Nic. Nic held still and let it happen. His gaze wouldn't waver from Kenneth's face. This wasn't the same man he had watched on the public stage and hated. Nic couldn't explain that thought, but he believed it to his core. Something had happened in those months he had been missing. He had reappeared as someone else. Someone Nic craved more than his next breath.

Bare from the waist up and with his pants resting below his hips, Nic sat on the bed and waited for Kenneth's next move.

Kenneth opened the bedside drawer. "Hopefully, there's some lube and condoms here."

The words barely penetrated Nic's overwhelmed emotions. "If not, there's some in my bag. Whose house did you say this was?"

"My best friend's, Jared. Well, my only friend, really."

"Just friends?" It seemed odd for Kenneth to feel confident enough to search the man's bedside drawer.

A wry smile touched Kenneth's lips. He closed the drawer. "Yes. I'll grab your bag."

Nic stared at nothing as Kenneth disappeared through the door. He had sounded so fucking jealous, even to his ears. Nic couldn't explain what had just occurred. He hated another man's name on Kenneth's lips. Nic didn't understand what was happening to him. Kenneth was back with Nic's bag in tow before Nic experienced a full meltdown.

He had to act to save himself. Nic needed to take back control. He shot to his feet and quickly stripped away the rest of clothing. "I need a moment. Is this the restroom?" Nic barely spared the room a glance as he shut himself inside. Thankfully, it was the bathroom because Nic hadn't truly checked before running for his life. He caught his reflection in the mirror and froze. His eyes were wild—like a trapped animal's. Nic turned on the water and splashed his face. What the fuck? He had really darted into the bathroom like a panicked teen. Kenneth had probably put his shoes on and had his keys out, ready to take Nic back home to his mom, where he belonged. Jesus. Things had just felt too real for a second. He fought a hysterical laugh.

Nic covered his eyes for a second and then dropped his hand. He looked down at his hard dick. For the first time in his life, Nic didn't believe he was only thinking with his cock. He wanted more with Kenneth fucking Yearly. Fuck it. Nic threw open the door. He found Kenneth beneath the covers, waiting.

Kenneth held up a tube of lube and a condom. "I found your stash."

"Good." Nic crossed the room, determined. He climbed onto the bed and claimed Kenneth's mouth. When he slid beneath the covers, he found Kenneth nude. Everything inside him relaxed. The tension bled from him. He was where he was meant to be. His fingers encircled Kenneth's erection. A breath stuttered through their kiss as Nic tugged.

"Put that condom on me."

Kenneth tore into the condom with all the impatience Nic felt in his heart. Nic shifted onto his knees so Kenneth could work. Kenneth rolled the condom down his length. Nic fought a moan at Kenneth's touch.

"Crack open that lube. I want to watch you play with that hole. Get it ready for me."

Without an ounce of hesitation, Kenneth squirted lube onto his fingers and drew up his knees. Nic watched Kenneth finger his hole, stretching it open for Nic. Nic's hunger grew by the second.

"I know you deserve all the foreplay in the world, but I've already jacked off once to the image of you. If I don't have the real thing right now, I can't promise I'll be gentle later."

"I didn't ask you to be gentle."

Nic tore his gaze away from the sexy show to meet Kenneth's stare. "I know, but that's what you deserve. If anyone says or acts otherwise, they don't deserve you. I want to be worthy of you."

Kenneth's shocked expression made the confessions worthwhile. Nic used his moment of distraction to lead his throbbing dick to Kenneth's waiting asshole. He didn't give Kenneth time to tense. Nic thrust.

A long, deep moan vibrated from Kenneth. Nic nearly came at the sound. He had to have more. Nic held Kenneth's legs in place and put his back into it. He thrust and rocked, riding Kenneth's ass. Nic had a hard time keeping his eyes open. The pleasure was too much. Kenneth felt amazing. He forced his eyes open. Nic stole a moment to appreciate Kenneth's body. He looked damn sexy. Nic was jealous of how well he had held up with age. In fact, they looked to be the same age. There didn't feel like there were any differences between them while Nic's dick sawed in and out of Kenneth's hole. They felt perfect.

Kenneth reached above him and grabbed the headboard. He met Nic stroke for stroke. Kenneth openly took the cock he craved.

"Fuck. Yes. Right there. Don't stop. Make me blow cum all over you."

Nic lost all sense of reason. He thrust faster. His balls got tighter. The pressure climbed higher. He turned greedy. Nic needed the tight heat to milk him into oblivion. He wanted to pump the man full of cum. It didn't matter a condom would stop that. Nic was beyond thinking straight. He needed the orgasm Kenneth's body promised.

Kenneth grabbed his dick and tugged. A cry rent the air. Cum hit Nic's chest. Kenneth's body squeezed him and then tried sucking him deeper. Nic lost his breath. Everything inside him tensed and then exploded into blinding pleasure. He moaned out his pleasure as he thrust hard and deep, letting Kenneth's body stroke every drop of cum from him. Nic didn't stop until the last wave subsided. Then he collapsed, seeking Kenneth's mouth. Their tongues stroked. Their fingers linked. It was like they clicked like puzzle pieces. Nic didn't run away from the feeling. He knew the truth. Nic wanted this. He wanted them.

CHAPTER FIVE

THERE WAS A SURE knowledge in Kenneth's gut some mistake had been made. Nic didn't feel wrong to him, but something had definitely shifted between them. It felt ready to strike and level him. There was some danger just out of sight. It had Kenneth's sixth sense screaming.

He was skating a fine line by bringing Nic to the home he enjoyed before becoming Kenneth. But he wanted Nic alone, and he had to be in Massachusetts this weekend. It wasn't like he could take an FBI agent to stay with a crime lord. Still, Kenneth risked everything for this.

"You could've stayed in Journey's old cabin for the weekend."

Kenneth tried keeping his gaze locked on the plans they were going over for Archer's new warehouses. Archer's bodyguard Cree, and Bryson—one of the biggest land developers in the country—made a show of not listening. Kenneth answered, as if they talked about the weather.

"I know. With the divorce, the media is in a frenzy. I thought it best to keep as much distance as possible. Who knows when a camera will appear in my face?"

Archer didn't respond immediately.

Kenneth lifted his chin. Their gazes collided.

Archer didn't look appeased. "So you chose to stay at the house of your former identity. Isn't that a risk in itself?"

Kenneth held Archer's stare, refusing to be cowed. Archer needed him more than Kenneth needed Archer. The most Archer could do was kill him. Kenneth didn't fear death. "Not at all. Jared had no ties to you or any crime. On paper, he was as clean as they come."

"True."

At Archer's seeming agreement, Kenneth returned to working on his pitch for his constituents.

"But is it not equally risky to bring that FBI agent with you?"

Everything inside Kenneth froze. Still, he couldn't show Archer any weakness. It was important he didn't give Archer a reason to harm Nic. "You have the FBI handled.

In fact, you have Nic reined in, but it's not enough. Everyone has seen us together now. If he actually uncovers anything at this point, the world will paint him as a scorned lover. Never doubt that I'm playing chess while everyone else plays checkers."

"Does that include me?"

"Why are we having this discussion? We have work to do." Kenneth didn't as much as blink as he waited for Archer's answer. Archer could strike like a snake at any point. He wasn't a man people crossed.

Archer's intelligent brown gaze moved over Kenneth's face, as if searching for the deceit. "You're right. I have plans with my husband, and you need to learn this."

Kenneth dipped his chin. "I'm good if you want to cut out and be with Angel. The three of us have this."

Bryson and Cree nodded.

Cree spoke up on his behalf. "Kenneth won't let us down. You can trust us to do this. Angel is more important."

With a final glance between them, Archer stood, leaving them alone without argument.

Bryson waited until there was no sign of Archer's return. "You'll get that boy killed."

Kenneth looked at the man who had signed his life over to Archer for some of the biggest land deals in years. His amber eyes didn't have as much fear as they should have. Unfortunately, he would learn. "I disagree. Nic's bull-doggedness will get him killed if I leave him unchecked. I have things under control."

Cree stepped in again. "I've known you for years. You have this. I have no doubts."

Before Kenneth could respond, his phone buzzed. He checked the face. At the sight of Nic's name, he opened the message.

Nic: *TOY*

Kenneth bit his lip to keep from smiling. He quickly texted back.

Kenneth: *Interested. What kind of toys?*

Nic's response came every bit as quickly.

Nic: *LMFAO!! TOY stands for thinking of you.*

Kenneth: *Still interested. I'm partial to anything that vibrates.*

Nic: ***rolls eyes***

Kenneth: *Still interested, though.*

"Oh, shit. You really are going to get this guy killed."

At Cree's words, Kenneth realized he was smiling like an idiot at his phone. Kenneth quickly hid his expression and put his phone away. He wouldn't. Not if he could help it. Kenneth liked Nic. They were more than a weekend fling. Kenneth just didn't know how much more yet. No matter what, though, he wouldn't let anything happen to Nic. He had things under control.

It was slightly uncomfortable hanging out in some stranger's house all day alone. Nic didn't want to snoop too much. He imagined a place this expensive had cameras everywhere. Instead, Nic spent most of the day staring at the TV and overthinking. No matter which way he turned things in his mind and inspected the situation, Nic came to the same conclusions. He was happy. Nic regretted nothing. He genuinely liked Kenneth. Nic wanted more.

He had texted Kenneth halfway through the day. Kenneth's responses had left him smiling all day. When the door beeped, alerting him Kenneth was home, Nic had to stop himself from jumping to his feet and rushing to the door like an excited kid. Then Kenneth stepped into sight and Nic couldn't fight his huge grin.

Kenneth lit when he saw Nic, as if a fire had ignited inside him. "Hey."

"Hey."

Kenneth took off his suit jacket and tossed it aside. "What have you done with your day?"

"You're looking at it."

"I'm sorry. I didn't mean to leave you bored all day. My meeting wasn't supposed to last so long."

Nic shrugged. He sat forward as Kenneth neared the couch and snagged Kenneth's hips. Nic towed him forward. "It was a relaxing day. But now that you're here." He dragged Kenneth into his lap.

Heat flashed in Kenneth's eyes as he straddled Nic. "What can I do for you?"

"You can tell me about your day and then you can tell me what you want for dinner."

"Except for an amazing text I got in the middle of my meeting, my day was boring. For future reference, my days are always boring. I don't have an exciting job like the FBI."

Nic couldn't stop smiling. "For your information, most days at the FBI are boring too. Especially now that I've essentially been demoted to the FBI's equivalent of a beat cop."

Kenneth's gaze moved over Nic's face. He looked like he genuinely cared about Nic's confession. "I could talk to someone. You shouldn't have been demoted over me."

Nic ran his hands up Kenneth's back because he couldn't stop himself. "No. I care a little less every day. If I was so easily set aside, then maybe it's no longer the job for me."

A deep line appeared between Kenneth's eyebrows. "Don't say that. You worked hard for them."

"Exactly, and they don't appreciate it. So I won't give my all any longer. I've given up a lot of weekends and free time for a job. That's all it is. Just a job. I'm not doing that anymore. My focus is on being happy now."

Kenneth bit his bottom lip. He looked a bit unsure of himself, as if he didn't know how Nic would react if he shared his thoughts.

"What? Say whatever you're thinking."

"I was thinking I could make you happy."

Nic held his breath.

Kenneth kept going. "Keep seeing me past this weekend."

Nic cleared his throat. He didn't want any misunderstandings. "Like exclusively?"

Kenneth flashed a pained smile, as if he expected he would get shot down. "Preferably, yes."

Nic's fingers found the knot in Kenneth's tie. He loosened it. "I'd like that. My only concern is you're going through a divorce. I don't want to be your rebound."

A snort burst from Kenneth so hard, it sounded like it hurt. "Wendy and I were married in name only."

Nic froze. "So the two of you never..." He couldn't finish that question. It felt way too intrusive.

"No."

"Like never, ever."

"Not once."

He was perplexed and curious as hell. "You two were married for a while."

"She married me for the money. I married her to keep up appearances. She said, after her first husband passed, she discovered she had no desire to share another man's bed, but she enjoyed my company. After we married, she didn't even get that much, nor did she care. She enjoyed a life of leisure and luxury."

"Then why the divorce?" Nic hated to keep prying, but he wanted to know everything about Kenneth.

"I embarrassed her. She made my life hell for it. It was best we went our separate ways." Kenneth's words sounded wooden. He tensed, as if he meant to climb from Nic's lap.

Nic stopped him by popping the first button on Kenneth's shirt. He kissed the skin he bared. "I'm sorry for prying." He slipped another button loose and nibbled Kenneth's neck. "I'd love to know I'm the only one in your bed."

"Done." Kenneth's breathless voice had Nic fighting an evil smile.

"You never told me what you want for dinner."

Kenneth snagged Nic's jaw and forced him to meet Kenneth's stare. "You." His mouth covered Nic's. Their tongues clashed. Nic's head spun as all his blood rushed to his cock. Before he recovered, Kenneth slithered to his knees between Nic's feet.

"Don't stop me this time."

The words barely registered before Nic's dick was in Kenneth's mouth. A cry tore from Nic as he slid down Kenneth's throat. Nic hadn't been ready. For a man who had spent years in the closet and fighting his sexuality, Kenneth had the most talented mouth Nic had ever encountered. He couldn't think. Kenneth tried sucking out his soul. Nic alternated between grasping at the couch and burying his fingers in Kenneth's hair. He kept lifting his hips, trying to match the pace. It was more of a squirm and flop because he was too big of a mess to do anything competently except beg. The suction on his dick had Nic saying words that didn't even make sense. His balls were already tightening. Pressure beat at his crown, trying to escape. If he had ever come more quickly in his life, he didn't recall it. Kenneth's skill left him embarrassingly weak.

Another loud cry ripped from him as the pressure finally exploded into pleasure. Moaning gasps wouldn't stop leaving his lips as he pumped Kenneth's mouth full of cum. Kenneth didn't stop sucking. Nic couldn't breathe properly. Spasms rocked him to the core. When his breathing finally steadied, Kenneth nuzzled his cock before pushing to his feet.

"I'll grab my phone and we can pick a place to eat together."

Fuck that. Nic Higgins did not leave a partner dissatisfied. In a flash, Nic was on his feet. He snagged Kenneth's waist and hauled him back to the couch. A laugh burst from Kenneth as Nic tore at his clothes. Something wild and primal rose inside Nic. He needed Kenneth to blow. Nic didn't stop frantically trying to get closer to Kenneth until he had Kenneth ass up and Nic's tongue was buried inside Kenneth's asshole.

"Oh, God."

An evil-sounding chuckle rumbled from Nic at Kenneth's cry. He went to work. Nic fingered Kenneth and played with his balls and dick. He licked and stroked. Nic gave his all. He let Kenneth's cries and whimpering lead him. Nic didn't stop until Kenneth was a quivering mess and his cum soaked the couch. Then a roar of satisfaction rang through Nic's mind. They were good together. They would be happy.

CHAPTER SIX

LIFE AND WORK WERE mundane as hell after such an amazing weekend. Nic tried focusing on his case, but his mind kept wandering back to Kenneth. The way Kenneth had kissed him when they parted ways kept getting stuck on repeat inside his head. He had never tasted so much promise. Nic fought the urge to call or text. He felt needy as hell.

"Here are the results on those fingerprints."

Nic startled at the interruption. As he reached for the file, he almost asked what case they were for until it hit him. He had forgotten about taking fingerprints from the vase of the flower Kenneth sent him. With a smile, Nic sent the junior detective on his way. Since he felt dumb for the impulsive move, Nic considered throwing the results in the trash without looking. If he got busted using company resources on a personal matter, he would be out the door. He was already on his last leg. In the end, curiosity won. There were three sets of fingerprints. None of them matched Kenneth. He hadn't personally delivered anything. That made sense. Delivering flowers wasn't something a senator would do.

Before Nic closed the file, one name caught his eye. Jared Wrought. There were likely countless Jareds in the world. It just seemed odd. They had just stayed at a Jared's house. Nic searched the name in the database. A picture appeared. Nic barely spared it a glance in favor of reading the details. The address was the home where they had stayed. Why had he been in DC? Had he delivered the flower? That was odd as hell. Nic checked the origin of the fingerprints. He was licensed to carry concealed. Thankfully, it wasn't due to an arrest. Nic's gaze moved back to his picture. He shared an odd resemblance to Kenneth. Maybe they were related. Kenneth had said Jared was his only friend. A lot of people had best friends that were also family. He could probably dig and find out, but he would definitely be fired if anyone caught him searching for anything else about Kenneth. Not to mention, that was a little too crazy, even for him.

Nic closed the search. He needed to turn off his detective brain before he ruined a good thing. Kenneth was amazing. Nic would not fuck things up by being intrusive.

"Director Stevens would like to speak to you in his office."

Fuck. Nic managed a fake smile. "Thank you." He couldn't shoot the messenger. Nic powered off his computer and headed for the boss's office. He gave a perfunctory knock before heading inside. "You wanted to see me?"

Stevens waved Nic inside. "Yes. Please have a seat."

Nic moved to the chair across from Stevens' desk and took a seat. "What can I do for you?"

A bland smile touched Stevens' lips. "How have things been with you?"

Nic spent a second wondering if it was a trick question. In all his years of working there, he didn't think the director had ever asked him that. "Good, and you?"

Stevens ignored his question. "That's good. We've been reviewing your credentials and discussing your future a lot lately."

While Nic had no idea who "we" was, he nodded.

Stevens never broke eye contact, as if he watched for any discomfort on Nic's behalf. "You've worked too hard to be where you are currently. It's a waste of talent." If Kenneth had spoken to someone on his behalf, Nic would fly off the handle. "But you've proven we can't move you higher here." Fuck. At least Kenneth hadn't spoken to anyone. "So, we've decided to move you back to lead investigator in Albuquerque."

"New Mexico?" Yes, it was dumb. He heard himself.

Stevens nodded. "They've been notified, and an office is being cleared for you. You have a week to settle things here and then

you'll report to your new position. Obviously, this comes with a raise and improved
benefits. Congratulations on your promo-
tion."

"No." Even Nic blinked at the immediate
decision.

Stevens' eyebrows rose. "What do you
mean, no?"

Nic stood. "I mean no. Consider this my
one-week notice since that's how long you
planned to have me here. It's been nice
working for you." That wasn't strictly true,
but he wouldn't be an ass.

Nic headed for the door.

"Nic."

Nic didn't turn. He kept going. Everything
had been said already. All his recent worries
and thoughts on his future had finally been
proven as real concerns. He had a week to

figure out what the fuck he would do now. Whatever he decided, it wouldn't be in god-damn Albuquerque. He was done.

Per usual, Kenneth made it through the workday by barely listening and daydreaming. He relived every moment he spent with Nic over the weekend. Kenneth cringed at every lie he had told. Things were getting deep. He didn't know how to keep his head above water any longer. The smart thing to do would be to never see Nic again. That didn't even feel like an option. He didn't know how to keep any of this going. Kenneth's phone buzzed with an incoming text, saving him from his raging thoughts. He smiled as soon as he saw Nic's name.

104

Nic: *Can I see you?*

Kenneth checked the time. The night's session was set to end in ten minutes. He couldn't fucking wait.

Kenneth: *Absolutely. My place? I'll text King so he can keep an eye out for you, in case you beat me there.*

Nic: *That's fine. I'll see you soon.*

There was something curt about Nic's messages that sent all Kenneth's alarm bells clanging. He didn't have the patience to wait to find out if everything was about to blow up in his face.

Kenneth: *Is everything okay?*

Nic: *Not really.*

Fuck. Kenneth's anxiety shot through the roof. He stood and headed for the door. No one tried stopping him or even sent him an odd look. It wasn't unusual for members to skip out early or even not show for the day. He had been trying to keep up the prior Kenneth's staunch discipline of being ever present. Today, he had better things to do. Leaving a few minutes early also meant he missed a ton of traffic. Still, Nic's car already sat parked in the circular drive out front. Kenneth headed for the garage and parked. He tried retreating into the cold Kenneth persona he had practiced for months before stepping into the senator's shoes. His pulse beat loudly in his ears. As he came through the door, King met him and took his coat. They exchanged a glance. King's silent stare said it all. Things with Nic weren't good.

With his heart in his throat, he went looking for his man. Kenneth found him outside, pacing by the pool. With his emotions on lockdown, he stepped outside.

"What's wrong?" Kenneth hadn't meant to skip all niceties and sound so cold, but he was a wreck inside.

Nic spun and met him halfway. Before Kenneth knew what to expect, Nic's mouth covered his. The kiss turned heated fast.

Kenneth was the first to pull away, but he kept his grip on Nic's t-shirt. "Tell me what's going on?" He sounded breathless. It couldn't be helped. Nic got him hot faster than anyone ever had before.

"They told me today they're transferring me to Albuquerque."

Everything inside Kenneth recoiled at the idea. Unfortunately, a sliver of good sense told him it was for the best. Thankfully, his shock saved him from saying anything stupid.

"So, I quit."

Kenneth was wrong. That was the best-case scenario. "Wow." Kenneth cleared his throat. He didn't know what to say. "Wow." He didn't know why he couldn't stop saying that.

Nic nodded. "I know. Honestly, I don't even know what happened. One second, the bomb dropped, and the next, I was just like, 'no.'" A hysterical-sounding laugh escaped Nic. "What the fuck am I going to do?"

Kenneth hauled Nic into his arms and held him. For a moment, they stood there in silence while Kenneth placed light kisses on Nic's temple. Kenneth needed a second to think. He didn't know how to fix this. Kenneth needed more info.

"Why don't we go inside, grab some wine, and discuss all your options? We'll figure this out."

Nic nodded.

Kenneth linked fingers with him and led him inside. Together, they chose two bottles of wine from Kenneth's collection, grabbed two glasses, and cuddled on the couch together. Kenneth waited until after they had each finished half a glass before picking a place to start.

"I apologize in advance, but I'm about to be intrusive as hell. Do you have any money in savings?" Kenneth really hoped Nic hadn't quit this job on a whim with nothing to his name. He would help him, but he doubted Nic would take the offer well.

Nic nodded. "I'd been saving up to buy a house, so I'm not completely broke."

That was good. "Is there anything else you'd like to do beyond the FBI?"

Nic stared at nothing. He looked lost. Kenneth wasn't sure he had heard the question. For a moment, Kenneth simply stared at Nic. This was his fault. All of it. If the day ever came that Nic learned the truth, he would hate Kenneth. Honestly, Kenneth hated himself enough for the both of them. This was supposed to be a simple slice out of time. A few years of work. No one was meant to get hurt. Kenneth rubbed his chest. He downed his wine. Over the years, Kenneth had done a lot of bad things. He had killed people, stolen cars and money. But all those jobs had been pulled on bad people. Nic was a good man. He didn't deserve this. Kenneth poured himself a second glass, hoping to drown his guilt.

"He said Albuquerque, and all I could think was I couldn't leave you. How crazy is that?"

Kenneth froze, with his glass lifted halfway to his mouth. He didn't know what to say.

Nic met his stare. "Why couldn't I leave you?"

They didn't look away from each other.

"Tell me to go to Albuquerque."

He should. Kenneth couldn't. The words wouldn't form. Nic would be better off there. They would be over and there'd be no chance of his lies being exposed. But it was like Kenneth's throat stopped working. He couldn't say the words.

"It was only a weekend," Kenneth said instead, hoping to convince himself.

Nic nodded. "I know."

Kenneth sat forward and set his glass on the coffee table. He swiped his hand over his eyes and then stared at the hardwood floor. "I should tell you to go. That's the right thing to do." As he said the words, an unexpected pain hit him in the chest. He had never felt the way he did about Nic with anyone else. They were friends, but they were also more. He couldn't explain it.

Kenneth felt good when he was with Nic. That wasn't a familiar state to Kenneth. He had been raised in Hell. All emotion had been stripped from him. Everything human had been stolen from him. Kenneth's eyelids dropped. He had to tell him to go.

Nic set his glass next to Kenneth's and scooted closer. His lips brushed the shell of Kenneth's ear. Air filled Kenneth's lungs. Kenneth twisted, and their lips met. In no time, they were a blazing inferno. They kissed and touched. Clothes slowly disappeared. With Nic pinned beneath him, Kenneth moved against him. The friction between their bodies had them gasping. Kenneth bit Nic's bottom lip and held on while he pleasured them. There was too much going on inside his head and heart. He just needed this moment out of time. The building pleasure cleared his head. He realized something massive. Nic was the only thing real in his life. His entire existence was shrouded by lies. He was surrounded by fake things and shady people. But Nic was real, and he mattered.

Kenneth kissed a path to Nic's ear. "I've got you. You're mine now. I won't let you want for a thing. Fuck those people who don't appreciate you. I do. You'll see. Stay and I'll give you everything."

Nic's ragged breaths drove him. So too did his desperation. Kenneth reached between them and held their cocks together as he thrust. Nic made a sound that nearly crippled Kenneth. He pumped faster. The pressure built. He couldn't hold back. Cum spit from his dick, soaking Nic's crown. Nic cried out. His cum mixed with Kenneth's. They held each other's stare as they fought for each breath. This couldn't be over for them. No matter what it took. They were way too real to turn back now.

Nic stared into the dark, seeing nothing but shadows as he savored the sensation of Kenneth's fingertips moving up and down his arm. Kenneth's heart beating steadily against his ear gave him life. Everything felt surreal as hell. He had shown up tonight, falling apart and desperate for anything Kenneth gave him. Now he felt like he floated on a cloud. Nothing touched him when Kenneth held him. He should be panicked and tearing out his hair. Instead, deep in his soul, he knew everything would be okay.

"When was the last time you had any time off?"

The question sounded groggy. Nic smiled. It was like Kenneth had been half asleep as he asked the question. "Last year, when my dad died. I took off for a week."

"Tomorrow, we'll grab your stuff. I have a yacht parked in Cape Cod. We'll stay there for a while. You need a break."

"Don't you need to work?"

He felt Kenneth shrug. "Everyone else always blows off session when they feel like it. No one will die if I do it for once."

"I've never been on a yacht. Maybe I'll get seasick." He hadn't ever been on a yacht, but he was mostly fucking with Kenneth. Kenneth had obviously chosen to take charge.

"You'll live. There're meds for that. I'll make sure you have them."

Nic hid a smile against Kenneth's chest, even though he couldn't see him.

"I felt that."

Nic's smile grew. "What?"

"That smile."

"I don't know what you're talking about."

Kenneth rolled, pinning Nic beneath him. Their lips automatically found each other in the dark. Kenneth pulled away. "I knew it."

"What?"

"You were smiling. I can taste it."

Another huge smile exploded across Nic's face at Kenneth's claim. "You can taste it?"

Kenneth kissed him again before answering. "Yes." Another peck landed on Nic's lips. "It tastes like oranges and sunshine." Kenneth kissed him again. "Mm-hmm. There's no doubt. That's it. We'll sail to Florida."

Nic shook his head. "Damn. You really do intend to take over my life, don't you?"

"You'll tell me to stop when I'm too much." Kenneth didn't wait for him to confirm or deny it. His mouth covered Nic's again.

A sigh rang through Nic's mind. How could he resist? Kenneth was right. He would know when things no longer felt right. That hadn't happened yet. He would get on that boat and go wherever Kenneth went. Crazy or not, he was happy. Maybe that would change soon. He hoped it didn't.

CHAPTER SEVEN

BEING VIRTUALLY ALONE—OTHER THAN their crew—with Nic on the open sea was so much better than Kenneth expected. Nic looked relaxed. Kenneth couldn't explain it other than Nic had lost the hard edge he always carried, as if a weight had been lifted from his shoulders. This was the level of freedom Kenneth wanted all the time. Unfortunately, the realization that this life was still years away kept sneaking up on him.

Nic's lips caressed the shell of his ear. His arms encircled Kenneth's waist. Kenneth savored the sensation of Nic's body pressed against his back. "What's on your mind? You look intense."

Kenneth stared at the water and tried to rearrange his features. "Just contemplating life."

"Share it with me. Maybe talking it out will help."

Kenneth turned in Nic's arms. "I plan to retire after this term."

Nic's eyebrows rose. "Really? I thought senators stayed until they died."

"Yeah, I don't want that."

"What do you want?"

Kenneth's gaze moved over Nic's face. "This."

Nic nodded. "I can see that. You look like you belong out here."

"That's not what I meant."

A deep line appeared between Nic's eyebrows. "Okay. Paint me a picture."

"I meant doing nothing all day. With you."

Nic's expression gave nothing away. "What are you saying?"

Kenneth didn't hold back. He needed Nic dependent on him. "Maybe don't look for a job right away."

A nervous-looking smile snapped to Nic's lips. "I can't just not work."

"Yes, you can. I can more than take care of you and I'm not saying it has to be permanent if you don't want. Just hang on to your savings. Let me take care of you, and if you decide you're bored or whatever, then look for something. You can take your time. Decide what you want the next phase of your life to be."

"You barely know me."

"Does it feel that way?"

Kenneth watched Nic's smile falter. Something flickered in his eyes, and Kenneth knew he wasn't alone. Nic felt their spark too.

Kenneth tried one more push. "The ball is completely in your court. This arrangement is only as permanent as you want it to be. But you know us old people. We can't waste any time."

Nic's smile exploded again. "You're not old. In fact, I think your grays have brown roots."

Damn. "Don't get your hopes up that I'll magically look younger. They'll turn gray."

"You're perfect the way you are."

"Say yes." Kenneth kept his voice soft, hoping to lure Nic into giving in.

"What will you give me if I do?"

He knew Nic was joking, but Kenneth wasn't. "Everything."

Nic leaned in and whisked his lips across Kenneth's. Kenneth's eyes fell closed as Nic did it again. "Yes."

Kenneth's heart soared. He wanted to shout his joy, but Nic kept stealing kisses.

"You should go below deck with me."

He fought a smile at Nic's suggestion. "Why?"

Nic brushed noses with him. "It's about to storm and you promised me everything."

Kenneth didn't need to hear more. He took Nic's hand and headed down the steps and into their private cabin. The yacht was gorgeous and tasteful. Just like everything the old Kenneth owned. Before stepping into Kenneth's shoes, he had never been on a yacht. Learning about yacht ownership had been one of the many ridiculous things Kenneth had to learn before taking the senator's place. No one understood how surreal and fake everything felt to him now. Nic was the only thing that kept him sane.

Nic overcame him, molding against his back as the first loud rumble of thunder rippled through the air. The boat rocked. Nic swept Kenneth into bed.

They kissed. Their fingers stayed linked. Nic didn't try for more. Kenneth's heart swelled a little more by the second. It was obvious all Nic wanted was to hold him and kiss. The backs of Kenneth's eyes burned. His throat tightened. In the midst of the biggest mistake of Kenneth's life, he had met the one. It would be a damn miracle if he didn't get him killed.

Two weeks alone with Kenneth had been amazing. It was odd, but Nic had never felt so close to anyone. They spent their days and nights talking and making love. They had so much in common. Nic never wanted to go back to reality. Now Kenneth offered to keep him in a dream life until Nic was ready to find a new career. Everything felt too good to be true. Maybe he was just blinded by the beautiful blossoming relationship they were building. It was possible the rose-colored glasses would fall away soon. For now, Nic felt crazy enough to jump in with both feet. After all, he had already quit his career. Nothing after that move seemed all that scary. He wanted Kenneth.

Nic knew he could strip away what little clothing they wore and bury himself inside Kenneth. As much as he loved doing that, his heart needed a different kind of closeness. Tomorrow, they would be back in Cape Cod. The day after that, they would return to DC. Some semblance of reality waited for them there. For now, he needed to cling to the bubble they had created on the ocean, where it felt like no one could touch them.

Nic settled on his side with his leg across Kenneth's thighs. He kissed and nibbled Kenneth's skin. "Tell me how you picture life when we get back to DC." Nic had to know. Kenneth hadn't been specific when he said he wanted to take care of Nic. Nic didn't know if Kenneth wanted to pay his bills or move him in, or what his thoughts were at all. He also didn't know how to ask all those questions without sounding like a gold digger. Nic wanted to know what he had agreed to do.

"That's up to you, really. As I said, the ball is in your court. But if you're asking what I'd prefer, then move in with me. If you're not ready for that, then tell me what you need to survive, and I'll make sure you get that every month."

Everything inside Nic recoiled at the idea of Kenneth sending him money every month like some sort of secret whore. He knew that wasn't the case, but just the thought of that arrangement filled him with rage. He already felt uncomfortable with Kenneth's offer. Nic couldn't choose the money option.

"My lease is month-to-month right now, since—like I said—I'd planned to buy a house soon. I didn't want to get tied to a long lease in case I found something I liked and wanted to move on it. So, it would be pretty easy to drop my apartment."

"Good." Kenneth sounded relieved. Nic felt his muscles relax.

"Are you worried about the rumors and drama this will cause? The ink is barely dry on your divorce papers. People will probably think you've been seeing me way longer than you have."

Kenneth shrugged. "I used to care what everyone thought. Then it almost killed me. Now I don't care at all. The only opinion that matters is my own... and yours, of course."

He was in so deep. Part of him really believed—when they returned to reality—everything would change. Nic would go back to his apartment. They would forget these crazy plans. It was the honeymoon phase. All this would fade. An unexpected laugh burst from Nic.

"We're completely insane." He met Kenneth's stare and found him smiling.

"Maybe."

They shared a smile and then burst into laughter. Nic had never been this happy. He had to see where it went. Maybe he would look back on these days with a deep mortification, but he would only live once. Right now, he wanted to live that life with Kenneth.

CHAPTER EIGHT

EACH DAY BACK AT work after coming back to reality got a little harder. Kenneth found himself less and less concerned about his role. It was all bullshit. The entire shit show was just that: a show. No one cared about their fellow man. They certainly didn't care about the people who voted them into their positions. Kenneth didn't listen most of the day. He played games on his phone and texted with Nic. Today was especially hard. While he worked, Nic packed his things and waited for the movers.

By the time they broke for lunch, Kenneth was ready to go screaming from the building. Unfortunately, the moment he stood; his phone buzzed with an incoming text from Cree.

Cree: *A car is waiting out back for you.*

Fuck. Kenneth had been expecting this, but a few days had passed. He had hoped he had dodged a bullet.

Kenneth: *On my way.*

He tucked his tie into his jacket and headed for the door without looking right or left. Kenneth couldn't risk anyone stopping him. Archer didn't like to be kept waiting. When he spotted the black SUV with Cree behind the wheel, he wondered if he would be seen again. He had truly been looking forward to going home to Nic tonight.

As he climbed into the back, he caught a glimpse of Archer's face. He didn't feel confident about how things would go. The moment the SUV moved; Kenneth knew he was in deep shit.

"Kenneth Yearly never missed a day of work until the day he went missing."

Kenneth nodded. "I'm aware."

Archer's hard voice didn't soften. "Kenneth Yearly didn't file for divorce even when his wife learned he was fucking her son."

"I know."

"Kenneth Yearly didn't play fucking games on his phone during session. He spent hours interrupting people to look like the biggest piece of shit alive."

"I remember."

Archer leaned his way and held his stare. "Then what in the fuck are you doing other than destroying everything we've set in motion?"

Kenneth didn't know how to respond. He had to keep Archer's attention away from Nic at all costs. Archer couldn't think for a second this was on Nic. If he did, Nic would disappear, and Kenneth would fall in line, or he would be next. "I'm finding it harder than expected to play the part."

Archer sat back. "You played the part just fine until this detective became a distraction."

Goddamn it. "I gave up literally everything for you, Archer. My face isn't even mine any longer. Having one goddamn thing that belongs to me is not a distraction. Me being nothing like Kenneth is the issue. I can't be both out as a gay man and spouting hate for gays. We agreed I would be a new, improved version of the senator. That means dating a law-abiding man and refusing to be baited by the wind bags. You hired me to get shit passed for you. I'm doing that. What else do you want from me?"

A muscle jumped in Archer's jaw. Kenneth fought the urge to plead his case. He wanted to bring up all the times he had killed for Archer. All the times he had kept Archer's man safe. He refused to speak. If Archer didn't know those things without Kenneth saying the words, there was no point.

"If you want to keep your new toy, maybe it's time we renegotiate."

Kenneth's eyelids dropped. There was no hope. Nothing he had done for Archer mattered. Like always, he would come out the loser.

Nic's patience was razor thin. It was almost time for Kenneth to get off work and the movers still hadn't arrived. Each time he called, they brushed him off, making excuses. He needed Kenneth to intervene, or nothing would get done. Nic had no idea how he had gone from being a strong, independent person to completely depending on Kenneth in no time.

Nic's phone buzzed. He juggled it in his rush to check his messages. It wasn't a text. His news app had a breaking news headline. Nic almost swiped away the notification without looking. He spotted Kenneth's name, but he wasn't quick enough to open the article. Nic growled in frustration as he desperately searched for the app through the countless apps he never used. Then, when he found it, the app didn't respond right away when he tapped it. Nic practically danced in place with irritation by the time it opened. He expected to have to search for the section on politics, but no. Kenneth was the top article of the day.

Senator Kenneth Yearly, the senator who famously went missing for several months, has been found dead at 57.

Nic's knees buckled. He hit the ground. His grip never loosened on the phone. His gaze never wavered from the article. He simply crumpled. Even though his brain didn't truly register all the words, Nic kept reading.

After not returning for the afternoon session, Yearly was found at two o'clock this afternoon in his car, unresponsive. He was transported to a local hospital where he was pronounced dead. Police say there were no visible signs of foul play. His cause of death is pending autopsy.

The phone dropped to the floor. Nic stared at nothing. There was no one to call. He felt like there was something he should do. Nic wanted to go to him—wherever he was—and check for himself. He wanted to see Kenneth's face one more time. But Nic was no one. He wasn't family. Nic knew how these things worked. He didn't matter at all. He was just the guy Kenneth had been dating. No one knew how close they had become. How special they had been. Nic glanced around at the packed boxes surrounding him. No one knew they were a case of love at first kiss.

Nic snagged his phone and settled on his side on the floor. He curled into a ball and opened Kenneth's messages. His vision blurred as he stared at all the loving and dirty words they had exchanged. They hadn't said the three that counted. Kenneth would never know Nic had fallen in love with him. It got harder to see as Nic's tears rolled unchecked, splashing onto the floor. Everything was gone. Nic had nothing but a howling emptiness and nothing else. No job. No home. No Kenneth. There was no warmth or comfort. Nic only had tears. In the blink of an eye, and without warning, he had lost everything.

Chapter Nine

NIC HADN'T BEEN ALLOWED to attend Kenneth's funeral. That had been a closed service. Instead, he had stood in line for the public viewing where he could pass Kenneth's coffin inside the Capitol. It was a closed casket. A huge flower arrangement covered the black, high-gloss surface. That was it. A few seconds of passing within feet of what could have been an empty coffin. That was all Nic got. Like everything else, the moment had felt hollow.

Since he had given up his lease, Nic had no choice but to move. He had transferred his things to a storage unit and found a hotel. Stevens had reached out and offered him his old job. With Yearly gone, the threat of Nic embarrassing them had passed. Nic had said he would think about it. He didn't want to accept, but he also didn't have the mental bandwidth needed to look for anything else. His heart wasn't in anything any longer. He just existed.

When several weeks passed and the fanfare settled down, and Nic was finally free to do so, he headed to Arlington. He found a quiet place to sit and just breathe. Nic didn't know how a person could be completely numb and still hurt, but he was there. A cool breeze skirted over his skin, hinting at the coming fall. He felt nothing. It was a beautiful day. Nothing felt real to Nic. It seemed like a million things had been left unsaid.

Yet he couldn't think of a single thing to say, so he sat in silence and stared at nothing. Kenneth was here, so he would be too.

Someone filled the spot next to him. Nic barely spared him a glance. He was huge and took up too much space. It was a bit irritating, considering there were benches everywhere. Unfortunately, Nic wasn't the bench police, and they lived in a free country. Still, Nic wondered if he would look like an asshole if he immediately moved benches. Then the guy leaned back and draped his arm across the back of the bench. That was too much. He looked the man's way and found the guy staring at him.

"What?" Nic hated to sound so aggressive with a stranger, but damn. His life was falling apart, and this dude was in his space.

"Kenneth wouldn't want you here."

"Wow." Nic had no idea why that was what fell from his lips, but he had nothing left to give anyone. This guy was in his space and lecturing about what Kenneth would want. Nic was too upset to wonder how the man knew about Kenneth and him. At the moment, the guy's words just felt like audacity. Before Nic could find the words to rip into him, the man reached inside the inner pocket of his suit jacket and pulled out an envelope.

"You don't know me, but I'm a friend of Kenneth's."

"Were a friend."

"What?"

Nic felt so fucking hollow. "You were a friend of his."

The guy shrugged as if tense didn't matter. "He gave me this to give to you." He handed Nic the envelope.

Nic's fingers wrapped around it. He felt closer to Kenneth the moment he touched the envelope. Nic wanted to scream for the man to leave him so he could see what was inside. He was equally afraid to look.

"What's your name?"

"Cree."

Nic nodded. "How did you know Kenneth?"

Cree's mouth lifted in one corner in a wicked smirk. "We go way back, but that's not important." He motioned toward the envelope. "That's important. Don't open it here. I'll walk you to your car."

Nic wanted to scream. He wasn't ready to leave. Everything that mattered to him was here. There was nothing left for him anywhere else. Why couldn't he have five minutes alone with his grief? But maybe Cree was right. If he opened this envelope and fell apart, he didn't want to do that here.

He stood. If there was any chance Kenneth left him a final letter, explaining why he had taken his own life, Nic needed those words. He had to be alone with the contents of the thick envelope he held. In silence, Cree walked beside him. Nic felt like he should ask questions. He had no energy to do so. The huge dark-haired man didn't invite conversation anyhow. He felt safe, though. That was odd. Kenneth truly felt like someone watched his back as he headed for his car. Nic lost himself inside his head, with no doubt Cree wouldn't let him fall.

"Do you have a last name, Cree?"

"Doesn't everyone?"

For the first time since losing Kenneth, Nic smiled. He deserved that answer.

"It's Erebus."

Nic's smile unexpectedly grew. "Greek God of the underworld."

A soft chuckle rumbled from Cree. "You can call me a Greek God if you want. I won't argue."

As they reached Nic's car, a hint of life returned to Nic's chest. It was barely a spark, but it brought the curiosity out in him. "Why did Kenneth entrust this job to you?"

"Because I understand," Cree said, and then kept moving, leaving Nic at his car. He didn't look back.

Nic watched him go until he completely disappeared before climbing inside his car. As much as Nic wanted to rip into the envelope, he started the car instead. With his heart in his throat, Nic headed for the hotel. He measured every breath and step as he made his way to his room. Nic felt like he rushed, but he didn't want to look hurried. Everything about his existence felt desperate since Kenneth died. He needed some semblance of control.

Once inside his room, Nic made it to the lone chair before ripping into the envelope. Everything froze inside him at the first glimpse of Kenneth's handwriting.

I can't even imagine how much you hate me right now.

The first written words immediately broke Nic. He sucked a ragged breath that sounded like his soul tore apart. That was it. That was how he felt, and he hated it. Kenneth had known Nic waited for him that day. They had made plans. Nic had given up everything for Kenneth. Kenneth had just given up. The anger was real. But he couldn't stop reading.

There's so much I wish I could explain. I won't leave it in a letter. No matter how things look right now, you should know I would never leave you in a lurch. I refuse to let Wendy try to claim my possessions, so I made ironclad arrangements for everything to go to you. The houses in Washington and New York have sold and there's a check for the balance included in these papers. The yacht is yours. My attorney will contact you on how to deal with its dock payments and all that. Being rich is complicated. He'll help you. I know you have questions, and this letter doesn't help, but you're a detective. In fact, you're the smartest man I've ever met. I love how your mind works. You'll figure things out.

Love, Kenneth.

It took everything Nic possessed not to rip the letter to shreds. Instead, he flipped to the next page. It was a check with more zeros than Nic had ever seen attached to his name. The next page was the deed to the yacht. Each page contained various info. Kenneth's lawyer. Instructions on how to go about depositing such a huge amount. Advice on how to make it last the rest of his life. It was a full-on instruction manual on how to handle sudden wealth.

Nic felt hollow. He sat back and stared at Kenneth's letter. Everything about it was odd. It wasn't a suicide note or a goodbye. It read as if it had been written this morning. Yet the attached documents read like something that took months to compile. Since Kenneth's death, Nic had wondered why. That was the biggest question. Why? They had been happy. Was it a cover up? Had Kenneth been diagnosed with some terrible disease the public wasn't privy to knowing? Had he been murdered? Fuck. The questions had his brain stuck in overdrive. Kenneth hinted at a mystery, and it was obvious he wanted Nic to solve it. It was maddening.

Nic read the letter again. This time, he did so with a detective's brain. Had the houses sold before Kenneth died? How long had he been planning this? Between the odd letter and some of the things Cree had said—like talking about Kenneth in the present tense—something didn't make sense. It wasn't uncommon for people to forget to talk in past tense when someone passed. He could overlook that, but the houses? That was odd.

He snagged his laptop and started searching. Property changing hands was a public affair. It was easy to find sale dates. He searched the address of the DC property. Then he chose a popular home site with past purchase info. Kenneth had bought the house in two thousand and two. It had been sold yesterday.

Nic sat back hard. He blinked at the computer. Maybe someone had been instructed to write the letter once the house sold. He had seen Kenneth's handwriting before, but he couldn't say if it was the same. Nic didn't have that much of a photographic memory.

With the curiosity bug stirred, Nic shot to his feet. He unplugged his laptop, grabbed the papers, and headed out. All his personal files from his FBI days were in storage. He needed to work.

The fifteen minutes it took him to drive to his storage unit were hell. A million thoughts and ideas ran through his mind. Puzzle pieces formed in his head. Kenneth was right. Nic would figure this out, even if it took him until his dying day.

At the unit, it was harder than expected to find what he needed. His entire life was crammed into one hundred and sixty square feet. Luckily, the Yearly files were in the same box as his fingerprint equipment because the handwriting on the letter—while close to Kenneth's—wasn't a complete match to the samples they had on file. Even though Nic knew he would likely be arrested if the FBI ever found out he had kept copies of the case files, he didn't care. He was beyond glad he had done so now. He had DNA results, fingerprints, and handwriting examples. Nic had everything he needed to study every aspect of Kenneth Yearly. He had obsessed over every nuance for much longer than necessary. All those days rushed back now. Nic was on the case again.

While the letter looked nearly identical to Kenneth's handwriting, the K was slightly different. People didn't change how they wrote the first letter of their name. Why would someone try to mimic Kenneth's handwriting? Nic dusted the letter for fingerprints. There looked to be only one set. He held the letter up to the copy of Kenneth's prints he had kept. They didn't match. The oddest idea hit. Nic tore through the files he had kept. There was only one official file he had sneaked from the building. He hadn't had time to copy it and he had used company resources for a personal matter, so really, he felt like the file belonged to him. Nic found the fingerprints from the vase. He held the letter against it and up to the light for comparison. They were an exact match: Jared Wrought.

Nic's mind went blank. Everything quieted. Jared was the one connection to everything. Nic had to find him. It was time they met.

Cree followed Nic to the hotel and then to his storage unit nearby. He sat outside and waited. When Nic had practically dashed from his hotel, Cree had known Nic was close to figuring things out. What the man did next would decide his fate. Cree didn't want to kill him. Jared would never forgive that. They had been friends for a long time. Cree didn't have many of those. But if Nic headed for FBI headquarters, Cree wouldn't have any other choice. Protecting Archer was his entire life. Nothing and no one endangered his boss and survived.

Nic backed from his parking space. Cree hung back so Nic wouldn't catch sight of him. Motion from the corner of his eye caught his attention. Cree looked to the left. The bay door stood open on a nearby storage unit. A young, twenty-something blond guy headed out with his head down while an older man yelled and threw shit behind him. Cree's eyebrows rose as a box hit the blond across the back. When he stumbled and turned, the older, dark-haired guy back-handed him. Cree blew out a breath. He had a GPS tracker on Nic's car. There was no real chance of losing him, but still. He didn't want to get involved in this shit. Cree couldn't look away. The blond was such a tiny thing. He didn't stand a chance against the older, much larger man. Then the guy hit the pixie with a closed fist. Cree sighed and dug his gun from the pocket inside the door. He honestly hadn't wanted to kill anyone today. That was a real shame.

CHAPTER TEN

NIC HAD NEVER BOOKED a flight so fast in his life. He had a huge check in his name now. There was no need to worry about spending part of his savings to get to Massachusetts. Nic also had no qualms claiming the trip was an emergency due to a death in the family to get a ticket at the last second. He had no clue what to expect in Massachusetts. For all he knew, Jared might not be there. After all, he had just had a letter delivered to Nic in DC. Nic had no clue what he had chased to this state. All he knew was he couldn't sit around and do nothing any longer. It had been weeks since Kenneth had been laid to rest. Nic only knew insanity now. He had to make this tragedy make sense. Otherwise, he might lose his mind permanently.

When Jared's house came into view, he immediately spotted two SUVs. Excitement and nervousness stirred inside him. Someone was home. Nic parked behind the dark blue SUV parked closest to the house. With a breath for courage, Nic stepped from his rental. He walked down the sidewalk to the front door. Each step felt a little wobblier. His breathing shallowed. His pulse pounded in his ears. He didn't know what he expected to find, but there was no going back. Nic rang the doorbell. Someone stirred behind the curtains closest to the door. Then the door swung wide.

"King?"

The behemoth who had worked for Kenneth stared out at him, looking unsurprised to see him. "Hey, Nic." He stepped aside, inviting Nic in without a single question.

Nic automatically stepped inside. Three men sat inside the living room with papers scattered across the coffee table between them, as if studying together. Nic recognized all of them. Archer Woods was a crime lord. Everyone knew it, but no one could prove anything. He was too good or too well-connected to get caught. Probably both. The man at his side was Jessie White: a longtime politician, and the man appointed to replace Kenneth. Then there was Jared. He was the only one Nic saw once their gazes met.

Archer and Jessie stood. They gathered the papers without acknowledging Nic.

"Take care of this, Jared."

Nic had no idea who said the words. He couldn't look away from Jared. His eyes were hazel. He was visibly younger without a trace of gray in his hair, but damn. Nic couldn't breathe.

The front door opened and closed.

Jared stood.

Nic swallowed. He couldn't remember why he had come.

"I knew you'd figure it out."

The voice was different, but they were so similar. "What did I figure out?"

Jared's gaze skirted away. His hands clenched and relaxed, as if he fought himself. "Oh. You don't..." Jared winced. When he did, his eyes crinkled in the corners for a second. Hyperventilation hit hard and fast. Nic couldn't draw a single breath deep enough to get oxygen to his brain.

Jared shot across the room and swept him to the couch. Nic found himself sitting with his head between his knees, sucking air.

"Just breathe." Jared rubbed his back.

To Nic's shame, tears sprang to his eyes. He knew that cologne. Those hands on his skin. He didn't understand what was happening.

Jared scratched his scalp and massaged his neck. "That's it. Just slow your breathing. I've got you."

Nic closed his eyes and tried to focus. He was so close to the truth. He couldn't break down now. Nic needed to understand. He wanted Kenneth.

Jared's heart pounded so fast, he thought he might faint. Nic was fucking brilliant. Jared had known he would find him. He wanted to kiss Nic. Hold him. It had been too long. Jared had withdrawals. Unfortunately, there was a damn good chance he would never get to have Nic again. He had told too many lies. Jared was the opposite of everything Nic stood for and believed. Nic could never love someone like him.

"What in the hell is happening?"

Honestly, Jared didn't know where to start. So, he went all the way to the beginning. "My mom gave birth to me when she was thirteen. She had been molested by her grandfather."

Nic sat up and met his stare. He still looked shellshocked, but he didn't look away from Jared.

Jared kept going. "I was pretty much hidden away until I was three and she started seeing signs I might end up enduring the same fate as her. So she dumped me at the nearest fire station. From there, I was shuffled from foster home to foster home while her grandfather stood trial. I think the courts hoped my mom would want me back when everything was settled. She didn't. I don't hold that against her. She had to do what she needed to do to survive."

"What does this have to do with anything?"

A sad smile tugged at the corners of Jared's mouth at the question. "Everything, because—eventually—I landed in an orphanage where I was sold."

"Sold?"

Nic sounded every bit as outraged as a good man should be. Unfortunately, Jared wasn't good and his feelings on the matter had been tortured from him too long ago to recall. "It's more common than you think. But I told you all of that to help you understand this; when you've had all the humanity stripped from you, there's nothing you're not willing to do to have a slice of peace."

"What did you do?"

A wry smile twisted Jared's lips. "Come on, Nic. Tell me you wouldn't know me in the dark with a dozen other people to choose from, because I'd know you."

Nic leaned back and covered his face. When his hands dropped, he looked wrecked. His gaze stayed locked straight ahead, as if seeing nothing. "Where is Senator Yearly?"

"He's dead."

Nic's gaze moved Jared's way. "How long has he been dead?"

"I imagine, since shortly after he went missing."

"So you didn't kill him?"

Jared shook his head.

"Do you know who did?"

Jared didn't respond. This wasn't going the way he hoped.

"Do you know who did?" Nic repeated louder.

"He got himself killed."

Nic stared at Jared.

Jared wanted to beg Nic to let him hold him.

Nic shook his head. "I don't understand."

He sounded so lost. Jared decided to rip off the bandage. "Kenneth Yearly was sleeping with his wife's son. He became so obsessed with the guy that he ended up dead. I was hired to take his place. It was a position I was meant to hold for six years until a permanent replacement could be found. But I miscalculated my tolerance for playing the part because I fell in love with you. Lying to you." Jared shook his head. "It was too hard."

Nic shot to his feet and buried his hands in his hair, making it stand on end. He paced. "I was right. The whole fucking time, I was right. I need to contact my old boss."

Jared's heart fell. "You underestimate how deep this goes."

Nic stopped pacing and met Jared's stare. "How deep?"

"You should cash that check and start a new life."

"No. I'll go to the Atlanta office. They have an entire division devoted to exposing people like Archer Woods."

"Do they, though?"

Nic looked like he was on the edge of desperation. "I can free you."

A sad smile pulled at the corners of Jared's mouth as he realized Nic's only concern was him. "My white knight." His smile fell. "I'll never be free. There are only two choices here: I can be a pawn alone or you can join me in my prison. No one leaves the family."

"Why did you do this to me?" Nic's whispered question sounded like it came from his soul.

Jared's lungs seized. A stuttered breath escaped him. Part of him had really hoped Nic would see Jared had chosen him. Archer could have killed them. Instead, he had given Jared this one shot at a life with Nic.

Looking at Nic now, Jared saw the truth. His lies had been too deep. He had cost Nic too much.

Jared cleared his throat. His voice still didn't work. He tried again. "Please cash that check. Kenneth Yearly was an evil, sadistic piece of shit. Nothing of value was lost when he died. I'm sorry I ruined your life. I should've tried harder to make you stay away. You just…" Jared swallowed. "You made me feel…" Jared tried to think of a way to describe what it had been like for him, meeting Nic. Not a single soul had ever wanted to keep him. He had never had what Nic offered: a home filled with real love. "For the first time in my life, I felt like I had a family. Thank you for that. I hope it's easy for you to forget me. I'll never forget you."

"You son of a bitch." Nic stormed toward Jared. "You clueless motherfucker." He straddled Jared's lap and kept coming. "I fucking hate you for this." His mouth covered Jared's.

Their kiss and connection were every bit as powerful as Jared remembered. In the last few days, he had begun questioning his sanity. He had been willing to die for this. Too much time apart had made him wonder if he imagined this wildly addictive heat. He hadn't. Jared couldn't hold Nic tightly enough. He couldn't stop touching him. Nic didn't understand how much Jared had sacrificed for a chance to keep him. Nic was worth it.

CHAPTER ELEVEN

JARED TASTED LIKE HIS Kenneth. When his eyes had closed, and their lips had met, Nic forgot all good sense. Nic wanted to tear off Jared's clothes. He wanted to kick his ass. How dare he? Yet so much made sense now. Nic had loathed everything about Senator Yearly. Maybe that was why he had fought so hard to find him. He had needed to prove to himself he would work as hard for a missing citizen he hated as he would for an innocent child. Nic had done that. He could be proud of his work. Nic had been right all along.

He had known the wonderful man he had gone to dinner with that first night couldn't be the same piece of shit who worked at the Capitol. Deep in his soul, he had felt it. Now he knew why, and he hadn't worked through his emotions yet. But Nic still loved the man beneath him, and he couldn't stop.

"I don't forgive you."

Jared nodded, looking every bit as turned on as Nic felt. "That's okay."

Nic went back to sucking Jared's tongue. He was so damn elated to have this again. Nic thought they had buried him with Kenneth. A part of him had died when he thought this man had.

"How fucking dare you break me the way you did?"

"It'll never happen again."

Nic believed. He didn't know why, but he knew Jared would never hurt him. Still, their issues weren't over yet. "This doesn't mean things are the same."

Jared kissed his neck. "Noted."

His body itched for more. "Take the ache away."

Jared stood, forcing Nic to his feet. He swept Nic down the hall so fast that everything was a blur. Their first time together came rushing back to him. They would make love again in the same place. This time, Nic wouldn't freak, even though he had more reasons now. He couldn't get out of his clothes fast enough. Every dream he thought had died was back. Nic needed to make it real.

With the bare minimum of clothes removed to get the job done, Nic took Jared down. Desperation clawed at his brain. He had to have this. Nic was convinced he wouldn't feel like Jared was his Kenneth until he buried himself root deep.

He lunged for the bedside drawer. Condoms, lube, and toys were inside. He grabbed what he needed. His hands shook. Jared jumped in to help. Together, they got Nic suited up and Jared's asshole lubed. Their erratic breaths told the story. They were equally ready to go insane if they didn't have this.

Nic fumbled his way into position. As he led his dick to Jared's asshole, their gazes met. The desperation fell away. A choking sound escaped Nic without permission. He rolled to the side and landed on his back. Nic covered his eyes as the tears hit. The shock had finally worn off enough to expose his raw feelings. He hurt. Deep to his core, he ached. Nic had thought he had lost the only man who he had ever truly loved. He had been sick with grief. Now those emotions couldn't stop pouring from him.

The bed shifted beside him. Jared straddled his body. He pried Nic's hands from his face. This time, when their gazes met, air filled Nic's lungs. He nodded. Even he didn't understand why, but it seemed Jared did.

Jared took Nic's cock. His heat engulfed Nic's erection. His gaze never wavered from holding Nic's stare. "I love you. Everything will be okay. I'll never let you be alone again."

Nic nodded again. This time, Jared kissed him. It was the sweetest of kisses, with lips brushing lips. A stuttered breath escaped Nic as Jared slowly rocked himself on Nic's cock. Their fingers linked. Nic lost himself to the pleasure. He savored the sensation of Jared riding him. Their skin felt good every place it touched. The most massive realization Nic had ever experienced overcame him. No low was too low. Nothing mattered to him except Jared. He should have realized it the day he quit his career simply because he couldn't leave this man. That should have been the moment he knew Jared could ask anything of him and Nic would be his man. No matter what face he wore or name he used, Nic loved the person who made love to him now. This man was his. For better or worse. Through good times and bad.

"I love you," Nic whispered between kisses. He felt Jared take a ragged breath. That one insecure-sounding breath brought Nic back to life. He would die for this man. Nic rolled, pinning Jared beneath him. He held Jared's stare. "If you ever pull any bullshit again without talking to me about it first, I'll fucking kill you myself."

"Deal."

Nic shifted positions. He needed to make Jared fly. "Good." That was the last coherent word either of them spoke. Nic slammed into Jared, taking what he wanted. He used Jared's body. His dick sawed in and out of Jared's ass. He watched it happen. The vision drove his lust. He needed to make Jared feel him for days. When his balls drew up tight, he didn't slow, even though Jared hadn't come yet. Nic was too in his feelings. He had to blow. Nic wanted to pump cum into Jared's ass, even if a condom stopped him. He needed this. Nic thrust faster and harder. The pressure built. Sounds burst from him with each thrust. They were primal. He didn't sound human any longer. When his orgasm hit, Nic cried out as he rode each wave. Even when the last twinge died, he wasn't satisfied. His insanity needed to be assuaged.

Nic pulled out and went down on Jared. Jared made a noise that burned into Nic's brain. Nic needed him to do it again. He sucked, bobbing on Jared's dick. Nic wasn't gentle. He didn't give Jared any quarter. Nic was all hands, fingers, tongue, and throat. He feasted. Jared was wild beneath him, squirming and begging. Cum filled Nic's mouth and still he didn't stop. He simply swallowed and kept sucking.

"Fuck, Nic. You're killing me. Goddamn. You could suck the rhinestones off a cowboy. Jesus. I'm dying."

An unexpected laugh burst from Nic. It felt good. Nic hadn't laughed since the last time he was with Jared. He nuzzled Jared's cock before kissing a path up Jared's body. When he reached Jared's sternum, he collapsed, squashing Jared beneath him. He didn't want to move. Nic couldn't. Jared might get away again if he did. That wasn't a chance he was willing to take.

Jared ran his fingers through Nic's hair and savored the moment. He had been terrified he would never get to hold Nic again. Every day without him had felt like a lifetime. To anyone else, maybe they hadn't been together long enough for him to be this obsessed. But when someone had never had anyone make them feel anything at all, they learned what was important very quickly. There had never been a single soul he had been willing to risk everything for before Nic. Since Jared had never known love, it had been ridiculously easy to spot.

"I don't understand how you look so different, yet still so similar."

Jared smiled at the ceiling, at Nic's mumbled words. "I already had similar features to the senator. A combination of surgery, colored contacts, and nonstop practice to mimic facial tics and mannerisms took care of the rest."

"I feel so stupid."

Jared forced Nic's chin up, leaving Nic no other choice but to meet his stare. "You're not stupid. You're the smartest man I know, and that's saying something. No matter what you think of the company I keep, these men are cunning as hell and they have the money to back their ideas. I was five foot nine. Now I'm six feet. I didn't even know people could get surgery to be taller. Unfortunately, I know now exactly how painful it is. The point was to make me completely indistinguishable from Kenneth. If you had figured things out before now, you'd be dead." He hated admitting that. Confessing that point meant exposing how much danger he had put Nic in by falling for him.

"I knew something wasn't right. I just didn't know what I knew."

Jared smiled. "I know." A ragged breath escaped him. "And you loved me anyway."

Nic moved higher and pressed his lips against Jared's. For a moment, they simply breathed each other's air. "I don't want to leave this bed. You have no idea how I've felt these last few weeks. But I know reality waits for us and I don't know if I'm ready to face it."

Panic shot through Jared. Nic had said he loved Jared and talked as if they would see more of each other, but he hadn't outright said they were okay. Maybe Nic was still done.

"I want to say I'll understand if you're done, but I can't."

Nic met his stare. The deep line between his eyebrows screamed anger and confusion.

"Goddamn. Do you still think I'd let you get away?"

"I'm sorry."

The line somehow got deeper. "Why in the fuck are you apologizing?"

Jared's throat swelled. "I don't know. I don't like it when you're angry."

Nic's expression cleared. "It's not you I'm angry with. It's the situation. We'll be fine."

"Will we?" Jared didn't know why he couldn't stop pushing. Everything still just felt so up in the air.

Nic settled between Jared's thighs. "You'll see." He went back to holding Jared as if he feared Jared would disappear. "Now, we're resting. I haven't slept for more than an hour at a time since you left me. I'm exhausted."

Jared kissed his forehead. "Close your eyes, baby. I'm not going anywhere." Jared stared at the ceiling and savored the moment. He honestly didn't know what would happen next, but he would give Nic a good life, no matter what it took. They were in this for the long haul. He wouldn't let anything tear them apart.

CHAPTER TWELVE

NEVER IN A MILLION years would Nic have imagined himself having dinner with Archer Woods. There was a lot of awkward silence. He got the feeling Archer tried to size him up, but Nic didn't make it easy. He had been living with Jared in Massachusetts for three months, and—in that time—he had always managed to not be home when Archer came around. Partially, it had been self-preservation, but mostly it was because Nic wasn't quite ready to accept reality. Finally, Archer had put his foot down and demanded this dinner. Nic knew it was now or never to be all in or out.

Angel, Archer's husband, was a huge bear covered in tattoos. Nic liked him. He looked every bit as uncomfortable as Nic. They kept meeting each other's stare and sharing a pained smile before going back to stare at their plates.

"Where's Cree?"

At Jared's question, Archer tossed a look Nic's way that screamed he didn't want to answer in front of him. "Indisposed."

"He brought home an injured stray a while back," Angel chimed in, sounding overly bright. "He's staying busy with that."

Jared's eyebrows rose. No one eased his obvious curiosity. They went back to eating.

Nic was used to living under pressure, but this was too much. He couldn't stand the silence. He stood. Jared stared up at him like he had lost his mind. Nic felt a thousand times better, all because he had Jared confused and off balance. He tossed Archer and Angel an apologetic look.

"Sorry for interrupting your dinner. I have to say something."

Archer gestured for him to continue, as if Nic had any intention of stopping anyhow. He had come this far. The love of his life had already suffered his entire life. Nic lived with that truth sitting on his chest all hours of the day. If there was any way Nic could make Jared's existence easier now, Nic would do it. Plus, he just fucking loved Jared more than anything else in the world.

Jared stared at him.

Nic couldn't let him worry. He dropped to one knee.

"Yes. He'll marry you. That's perfect. You can't testify against him in court, and I can stop worrying about this."

Nic's gaze swung Archer's way at his outburst.

Angel brushed Archer's jaw, bringing his gaze his way. "Baby, stay out of it."

"What? Between this and Cree…"

"You're ruining their moment."

Jared grabbed Nic's hand and stood. "We need to talk." He dragged Nic toward the door. Nic scrambled to his feet and followed. He was confused as fuck. This wasn't going at all as planned. He had thought this would fix everything. Jared didn't look happy. In fact, the moment they were outside and alone, he spun on Nic. "What the hell was that?"

Nic blinked. He hadn't expected this adverse of a reaction. "Nothing, I guess. I thought you might actually want to marry me. My mistake."

Jared looked genuinely upset. "Of course, I want to marry you, but I don't want to marry you just to please Archer. I don't want to spend the rest of my life wondering if you're really happy or just stuck. Damn, I already have to spend every day knowing I'm the worst thing that's ever happened to you. I've already taken everything else from you. Don't make me have to live with knowing you can never, ever walk away from a life I know you hate."

Nic was blown away. Jared hadn't shown an ounce of insecurity about their relationship since Nic decided to stay. He hadn't known Jared believed he didn't want to be here. "Do you really think I'm stuck?"

Jared shrugged in such a helpless way that was like getting punched in the chest. Nic would have never let Jared silently hurt like this for three months if he had suspected.

Before he realized what he would do, Nic overcame Jared, backing him against the door and trapping him. "Every time I've said I love you, did you think I was lying?"

"No, but—"

"Look at me and tell me I'm not serious about us."

"It's not that I don't think—"

Nic's control over his temper vanished. "I'm in love with you. From the first night we sat by the pool and talked for hours, I've known you're the one for me. No one makes me do shit. When I thought you were dead, I nearly lost my mind because it felt so wrong for anything at all to separate us. Do you really think I give a good goddamn about Archer?

I need *you* at peace. I need to know you're mine forever. This is about you and me. If you don't want me forever, then fine. But don't you fucking dare try to tell me I don't want you for the rest of my life because I do."

Jared took a ragged-sounding breath.

Nic wondered how Jared had ever gotten away with pretending to be a fifty-seven-year-old cold-hearted bastard. He looked incredibly young and vulnerable as he stared at Nic with his heart in his eyes. "I was supposed to be free when I finished my six-year term. When it was over, I'd planned to take that yacht and go. I'd planned to sail around the world and never look back at this life. But I fell in love with you and realized I love you more than the idea of freedom. I gave up that dream because I'd rather have you. Of course, I want to spend the rest of my life with you. Of course, I want to marry you."

Nic pulled the ring from his pocket and held it up between his fingers. "Then say yes."

"Yes."

Nic slipped the ring on Jared's finger, but he was still angry. Not at Jared, but at Archer. If Jared thought about it, genuinely thought about it, he would know Archer wouldn't have let him go when those six years ended. Jared had done too much. He was in too deep. Archer couldn't let that go unchecked.

After pressing a quick, hard kiss to Jared's lips, Nic took his hand. "Come on." He headed back inside and toward the table where Archer and Angel held each other's stare, looking ready to be alone for the night.

Nic picked up his glass and polished off the wine inside. "Thank you for dinner. Jared and I are headed to get married. If you need us afterward, we'll be on our yacht, enjoying a quiet life."

He set his glass on the table and headed for the door again with Jared in tow.

"Nic."

At Angel's shout, Nic glanced over his shoulder.

Angel smiled. "Congratulations."

Nic dipped his chin. "Thank you. It was nice meeting you." To Nic's surprise, he meant it. Angel seemed like a genuinely nice person. That meant Archer had to have some redeeming qualities buried in his cold heart. As long as they never lost touch, and Archer knew where they were, Nic didn't doubt he would let them have a quiet life. From what Nic had seen, he had already left them alone for the most part since Nic arrived in Massachusetts. The only time Jared had seen him had been when Archer pressed him for a permanent solution on Nic. Now he had one, and they planned to fall off the map.

It was the perfect outcome for everyone. Personally, Nic couldn't wait to start the rest of his life with Jared. That sounded like a dream come true.

The shock was thick. Jared kept waiting for it to wear off, but it wouldn't. After leaving Archer behind, Nic had gotten behind the wheel and driven them across the state line into Rhode Island where there was no waiting period to get married. Jared had repeated his vows with a sense of disconnect from reality the entire time. Then they had been back home, packing their bags.

Color and sound didn't truly return to Jared's senses until they stepped aboard the yacht Jared had ensured Nic had inherited.

Then it hit him he was truly married and Nic had gotten a bit screwed in the deal.

"You should've gotten a big wedding."

Nic glanced over his shoulder halfway through putting clothes in the dresser inside their private cabin. "Did you want a big wedding? We could always do that later."

Jared sat on the bed. It always took him a little while to adjust to the constant rocking of a boat. They were still docked and wouldn't set sail until they had a crew in the morning. Nic could still run.

"I don't need a wedding. It just hit me you should've had one. I wanted to give you more than a ring we picked up at the only place open and vows in front of some hippie who was half asleep."

A bright smile exploded across Nic's face. He dropped his chore and straddled Jared's lap. He kept coming until he had Jared on his back. "Big weddings are so stressful, I doubt anyone ever remembers much about them at all. But you'll always remember Tommy, the ordained surfer who smelled like weed and is the only chapel open from eight p.m. to two a.m., because that's when the tide matches his vibe."

A snort escaped Jared. Nic was right. He would never forget this night. It hadn't been the typical wedding, but they weren't the average couple. Everything about them had been wild since the moment they met. A unique wedding fit them perfectly.

"I love you."

Nic's smile never dimmed. "I love you too."

Jared's heart was full in a way he hadn't thought possible. He felt like he had been living in a slight panic for so many years, he didn't know how to be calm. Nic brought him peace. His throat swelled just thinking about it.

"I used to dream about having the kind of life you see on television and on Christmas cards. Before you, I didn't think anyone really had that life. I mean, Angel and Archer are deeply in love, but it's still a lot of Angel yelling at Archer to be human. Part of me thought—if anything—that would be me. Maybe none of us who survived hell can be completely human. Then you just sort of forced a normal life on me and I have never been more addicted to anything."

Nic lowered his head and kissed the tip of Jared's nose. "This is only the beginning." Nic kissed his cheek. "I plan to shower you in love and normalcy." He whisked his lips across Jared's mouth. "You'll beg me to give you peace." As Nic's mouth moved to Jared's neck, he imagined the only peace he would beg for was for rest in between rounds of lovemaking. They had lived together long enough for Jared to already know Nic had a ferocious appetite. He had never felt so wanted.

Nic's hand headed south. Jared's cock stirred. All stress and doubts scattered. His breathing deepened. Jared's body knew what Nic could do for it. He already couldn't wait. In the past three months, it felt like they had done nothing except talk and make love. They had been brutally open with each other in every way. While Nic had been more than a little shocked by the full story of Jared's past, he had loved him anyway. Jared hadn't thought anyone would love him. Nic's love felt twice as beautiful because of his pure acceptance. Together, they had lost and found so much. Even when things in Jared's life had been fake, they had been very real with Nic. He supposed Nic knew that.

Nic's mouth moved down Jared's body and he forgot to overthink everything. They had been beautiful together since day one. Jared knew they would still be perfect on day one million together. Nic had promised him they would be. That was all the reassurance Jared needed. He had Nic's vow to love him forever until death. Truthfully, Nic had already loved him past that point. No man could ask for more.

Keep an eye out for the next Damaged Devils, *Deviant Ways*.

Please consider leaving a review at the retailer where you purchased this book. Reviews really help with a book's visibility, which allows me to continue writing more stories. Thank you, Charity.

About the Author

CHARITY PARKERSON IS AN award-winning and multi-published author with several companies. Born with no filter from her brain to her mouth, she decided to take this odd quirk and insert it in her characters. One of her greatest loves is writing morally gray characters. You'll find them scattered throughout her hundreds of titles.

*Eight-time Readers' Favorite Award Winner

*2015 Passionate Plume Award Finalist

*2013 Reviewers' Choice Award Winner

*2012 ARRA Finalist for Favorite Paranormal Romance

*Five-time winner of The Mistress of the Darkpath

Connect with her online:

*Sign up for her newsletter: https://sendfox .com/charityparkerson

*Join her readers' group on Facebook: http ://bit.ly/CharitysTribe

*Website: https://www.charityparkerson.c om

*A list of her social media accounts and give-aways all in one place: http://hy.page/chari typarkerson

Content

Content Warning: Damaged Devils is a dark romance series that deals with dark subjects. There is murder, sexual assault, abuse, kidnapping, and power dynamic relationships. These are anti-hero books. They won't be for everyone.